David Poindexter's Disappearance
and Other Tales

Julian Hawthorne

Contents

DAVID POINDEXTER'S

DISAPPEARANCE AND OTHER TALES

BY

Julian Hawthorne

DAVID POINDEXTER'S DISAPPEARANCE.

Among the records of the English state trials are to be found many strange stories, which would, as the phrase is, make the fortune of a modern novelist. But there are also numerous cases, not less stimulating to imagination and curiosity, which never attained more than local notoriety, of which the law was able to take but comparatively small cognizance, although they became subjects of much unofficial discussion and mystification. Among these cases none, perhaps, is better worth recalling than that of David Poindexter. It will be my aim here to tell the tale as simply and briefly as possible --to repeat it, indeed, very much as it came to my ears while living, several years ago, near the scene in which its events took place. There is a temptation to amplify it, and to give it a more recent date and a different setting; but (other considerations aside) the story might lose in force and weight more than it would thereby gain in artistic balance and smoothness.

David Poindexter was a younger son of an old and respected family in Sussex, England. He was born in London in 1785. He was educated at Oxford, with a view to his entering the clerical profession, and in the year 1810 he obtained a living in the little town of Witton, near Twickenham, known historically as the home of Sir John Suckling. The Poindexters had been much impoverished by the excesses of David's father and grandfather, and David seems to have had few or no resources beyond the very modest stipend appertaining to his position. He was, at all events, poor, though possessed of capacities which bade fair to open to him some of the higher prizes of his calling; but, on the other hand, there is evidence that he chafed at his poverty, and reason to believe that he had inherited no small share of the ill-regulated temperament which had proved so detrimental to the elder generations of his family.

Personally he was a man of striking aspect, having long, dark hair, heavily-marked eyebrows, and blue eyes; his mouth and chin were graceful in contour, but wanting in resolution; his figure was tall, well knit, and slender. He was an eloquent preacher, and capable, when warmed by his subject, of powerfully affecting the emotions of his congregation. He was a great favorite with women--whom, however, he uniformly treated with coldness--and by no means unpopular with men, toward some of whom he manifested much less reserve. Nevertheless, before the close of the second year of his incumbency he was known to be paying his addresses to a young lady of the neighborhood, Miss Edith Saltine, the only child of an ex-army officer. The colonel was a widower, and in poor health, and since he was living mainly on his half-pay, and had very little to give his daughter, the affair was looked upon as a love match, the rather since Edith was a handsome young woman of charming character. The Reverend David Poindexter certainly had every appearance of being deeply in love; and it is often seen that the passions of reserved men, when once aroused, are stronger than those of persons more generally demonstrative.

Colonel Saltine did not at first receive his proposed son-in-law with favor. He was a valetudinarian, and accustomed to regard his daughter as his nurse by right, and he resented the idea of her leaving him forlorn for the sake of a good-looking parson. It is very likely that his objections might have had the effect of breaking off the match, for his daughter was devotedly attached to him, and hardly questioned his right to dispose of her as he saw fit; but after a while the worthy gentleman seems to have thought better of his contrariness. Poindexter had strong persuasive powers, and no doubt made himself personally agreeable to the colonel, and, moreover, it was arranged that the latter should occupy the same house with Mr. and Mrs. Poindexter after they were married. Nevertheless, the colonel was not a man to move rapidly, and the engagement had worn along for nearly a year without the wedding-day having been fixed. One winter evening in the early part of December, Poindexter dined with the colonel and Edith, and as the gentlemen were sitting over their wine the lover spoke on the topic that was uppermost in his thoughts, and asked his host whether there was any good reason why the marriage should not be consummated at once.

"Christmas is at hand," the young man remarked; "why should it not be rendered doubly memorable by granting this great boon?"

"For a parson, David, you are a deuced impatient man," the colonel said.

"Parsons are human," the other exclaimed with warmth.

"Humph! I suppose some of them are. In fact, David, if I didn't believe that there was something more in you than texts and litanies and the Athanasian creed, I'll be hanged if I'd ever have let you look twice at Edith. That girl has got blood in her veins, David; she's not to be thrown away on any lantern-jawed, white-livered doctor of souls, I can tell you."

David held his head down, and seemed not to intend a reply; but he suddenly raised his eyes, and fixed them upon the colonel's. "You know what my father was," he said, in a low, distinct voice; "I am my father's son."

"That idea has occurred to me more than once, David, and to say the truth, I've liked you none the less for it. But, then, what the deuce should a fellow like you want to do in a pulpit? I respect the cloth as much as any man, I hope, but leaving theory aside, and coming down to practice, aren't there fools and knaves enough in the world to carry on that business, without a fellow of heart and spirit like you going into it?"

"Theory or no theory, there have been as great men in the pulpit as in any other position," said David, gloomily.

"I don't say to the contrary: ecclesiastical history, and all that: but what I do say is, if a man is great in the pulpit, it's a pity he isn't somewhere else, where he could use his greatness to more advantage."

"Well," remarked David, in the same somber tone, "I am not contented: so much I can admit to the father of the woman I love. But you know as well as I do that men nowadays are called to my profession not so much by the Divine summons as by the accident of birth. Were it not for the law of primogeniture, Colonel Saltine, the Church of England would be, for the most part, a congregation without a clergyman."

"Gad! I'm much of your opinion," returned the colonel, with a grin; "but there are two doors, you know, for a second son to enter the world by. If he doesn't fancy a cassock, he can put on His Majesty's uniform."

"Neither the discipline nor the activity of a soldier's life would suit me," David answered. "So far as I know my own nature, what it craves is freedom, and the enjoyment of its capacities. Only under such conditions could I show what I am capable of. In other words," he added, with a short laugh, "ten thousand a year is the profession I should choose."

"Ah," murmured the colonel, heaving a sigh, "I doubt that's a profession we'd all of us like to practice as well as preach. What! no more wine? Oh, ay, Edith, of course! Well, go to her, sir, if you must; but when you come to my age you'll have found out which wears the best --woman or the bottle. I'll join you presently, and maybe we'll see what can be done about this marrying business."

So David went to Edith, and they had a clear hour together before they heard the colonel's slippered tread hobbling through the hall. Just before he opened the door, David had said: "I sometimes doubt whether you wholly love me, after all." And she had answered:

"If I do not, it is because I sometimes feel as if you were not your real self."

The colonel heard nothing of this odd bit of dialogue; but when he had subsided, with his usual grunt, into his arm-chair beside the fire- place, and Edith had brought him his foot-stool and his pipe, and pat the velvet skull cap on his bald pate, he drew a long whiff of tobacco smoke, and said:

"If you young folks want to set up housekeeping a month from to-day, you can do it, for all I care."

Little did any one of the three suspect what that month was destined to bring forth.

David Poindexter's father had been married twice, his second wife dying within a year of her wedding-day, and two weeks after bringing David into the world. This lady, whose maiden name was Lambert, had a brother who was a gentleman farmer, and a tolerably successful one. His farm was situated in the parish of Witton, and he owned a handsome house on the outskirts of the town itself. He and David's father had been at one time great friends, insomuch that David was named after him, and Lambert, as his godfather as well as uncle, presented the child with the usual silver mug. Lambert was never known to have married, but there were rumors, dating as far as back David's earliest recollections, to the effect that he had entertained a secret and obscure passion for some foreign woman of great beauty, but of doubtful character and antecedents. Nobody could be found who had ever seen this woman, or would accept the responsibility of asserting that she actually existed; but she afforded a convenient means of accounting for many things that seemed mysterious in Mr. Lambert's conduct. At length, when David was about eight years old, his godfather left England abruptly, and without telling any one whither he was going or when he would return. As a matter of fact he never did return, nor had any certain news ever been heard of him since his departure. Neither his house nor his farm was ever sold, however, though they were rented to more than one tenant during a number of years. It was said, also, that Lambert held possession of some valuable real estate in London. Nevertheless, in process of time he was forgotten, or remembered only as a name. And the new generation of men, though they might speak of "the old Lambert House," neither knew nor cared how it happened to have that title. For aught they could tell, it might have borne it ever since Queen Elizabeth's time. Even David Poindexter had long ceased to think of his uncle as anything much more substantial than a dream.

He was all the more surprised, therefore, when, on the day following the interview just mentioned, he received a letter from the late David Lambert's lawyers. It informed him in substance that his uncle had died in Constantinople, unmarried (so far as could be ascertained), intestate, and without blood-relations surviving him. Under these circumstances, his property, amounting to one hundred and sixty thousand pounds, the bulk of which was invested in land and houses in the city of London, as well as the country-seat in Witton known as the old Lambert House, and the farm lands thereto appertaining--all this wealth, not to mention four or five thousand pounds in ready money, came into possession of the late David Lambert's nearest of kin, who, as it appeared, was none other than the Reverend David Poindexter. "Would that gentleman, therefore be kind enough, at his convenience, to advise his obedient servants as to what disposition he wished to make of his inheritance?"

It was a Saturday morning, and the young clergyman was sitting at his study table; the fire was burning in the grate at his right hand, and his half-written sermon lay on the desk before him. After reading the letter, at first hurriedly and amazedly, afterward more slowly, with frequent pauses, he folded it up, and, still holding it in his hand, leaned back in his chair, and remained for the better part of an hour in a state of deep preoccupation. Many changing expressions passed across his face, and glowed in his dark-blue eyes, and trembled on the curves of his lips.

At last he roused himself, sat erect, and smote the table violently with his clinched hand. Yes, it was true it was real; he, David Poindexter, an hour ago the poor imprisoned clergyman of the Church of England--he, as by a stroke of magic, was free, powerful, emancipated, the heir of seven thousand pounds a year! And what about tomorrow's sermon?

He rose up smiling, with a vivid color in his cheeks and a bright sparkle in his eyes. He stretched himself to his full height, threw out his arms, and smote his chest with both fists. What a load was gone from his heart! What a new ardor of life was this that danced in his veins! He walked with long strides to the window, and threw it wide open, breathing in the rush of bright icy air with deep inhalations. Freedom! emancipation! Yonder, above the dark, level boughs of the cedar of Lebanon, rose the square, gray tower of the church. Yesterday it was the incubus of his vain hopes; to-day it was the tomb of a dead and despised past. What had David Poindexter to do with calling sinners to repentance? Let him first find out for himself what sin was like. Then he looked to the right, where between the leafless trees Colonel Saltine's little dwelling raised its red-tile roof above the high garden-wall. And so, Edith, you doubted whether I were at all times my real self? You shall not need to make that complaint hereafter. As for to-morrow's sermon--I am not he who wrote sermons, nor shall I ever preach any. Away with it, therefore!

He strode back to the table, took up the sheets of manuscript from the desk, tore them across, and laid them on the burning coals. They smoldered for a moment, then blazed up, and the draught from the open window whisked the blackened ashes up the chimney. David stood, meanwhile, with his arms folded, smiling to himself, and repeating, in a low voice:

"Never again--never again--never again."

By-and-by he reseated himself at his desk, and hurriedly wrote two or three notes, one of which was directed to Miss Saltine. He gave them to his servant with an injunction to deliver them at their addresses during the afternoon. Looking at his watch, he was surprised to find that it was already past twelve o'clock. He went up-stairs, packed a small portmanteau, made some changes in his dress, and came down again with a buoyant step. There was a decanter half full of sherry on the sideboard in the dining-room; he poured out and drank two glasses in succession. This done, he put on his hat, and left the house with his portmanteau in his hand,

and ten minutes later he had intercepted the London coach, and was bowling along on his way to the city.

There was a dramatic instinct in David, as in many eloquent men of impressionable temperament, which caused him every now and then to look upon all that was occurring as a sort of play, and to resolve to act his part in a telling and picturesque manner. On that Saturday afternoon he had an interview with the late Mr. Lambert's lawyers, and they were struck by his calm, lofty, and indifferent bearing. He seemed to regard worldly prosperity as a thing beneath him, yet to feel in a half-impatient way the responsibility which the control of wealth forced upon him.

"It is my purpose not to allow this legacy to interfere permanently with my devotion to my higher duties," he remarked, "but I have taken measures to enable myself to place these affairs upon a fixed and convenient footing. I presume," he added, fixing his eyes steadily upon his interlocutor, "that you have thoroughly investigated the possibility of there being any claimant nearer than myself?"

"No such claimant could exist," the lawyer replied, "unless the late Mr. Lambert had married and had issue."

"Is there, then, any reason to suppose that he contemplated the contingency that has happened?"

"If he bestowed any thought at all upon the subject, that contingency could hardly have failed to present itself to his mind," the lawyer answered.

David consented to receive the draft for a thousand pounds which was tendered him, and took his leave. He returned to his rooms at the Tavistock Hotel, Covent Garden. In the evening, after making some changes in his costume, he went to the theatre, and saw Kean play something of Shakespeare's. When the play was over, and he was out in the frosty air again, he felt it impossible to sleep. It was after midnight before he returned to his hotel, with flushed cheeks, and a peculiar brilliance in his eyes. He slept heavily, but awoke early in the morning with a slight feeling of feverishness. It was Sunday morning. He thought of his study in the parsonage at Witton, with its bright fire, its simplicity, its repose. He thought of the church, and of the congregation which he would never face again. And Edith--what had been her thoughts and dreams during the night? He got up, and went to the window. It looked out upon a narrow, inclosed court. The sky was dingy, the air was full of the muffled tumult of the city. His present state, as to its merely external aspect, was certainly not so agreeable as that of the morning before. Ay, but what a vista had opened now which then was closed! David dressed himself, and went down to his breakfast. While sitting at his table in the window, looking out upon the market-place, and stirring his cup of Mocha, a gentleman came up and accosted him.

"Am I mistaken, or is your name Poindexter?"

David looked up, and recognized Harwood Courtney, a son of Lord Derwent. Courtney was a man of fashion, a member of the great clubs, and a man, as they say, with a reputation. He was a good twenty years older than David, and had been the companion of the latter's father in some of his wildest escapades. To David, at this moment, he was the representative and symbol of that great, splendid, unregenerate world, with which it was his purpose to make acquaintance.

"You are not mistaken, Mr. Courtney," he said, quietly. "Have you breakfasted? It is some time since we have met."

"Why, yes, egad! If I remember right, you were setting out on another road than that which I was travelling. However, we sinners, you know, depend upon you parsons to pull us up in time to prevent any--er--any *very* serious catastrophe! Ha! ha!"

"I understand you; but for my part I have left the pulpit," said David, uttering the irrevocable words with a carelessness which he himself wondered at.

"By Jove!" exclaimed Courtney, with a little intonation of surprise and curiosity, which his good breeding prevented him from formulating more explicitly. As David made no rejoinder, he presently continued: "Then-- er--perhaps you might find it in your way to dine with me this evening. Only one or two friends--a very quiet Sunday party."

"Thank you," said David. "I had intended going to bed betimes to-night; but it will give me pleasure to meet a quiet party."

"Then that's settled," exclaimed Courtney; "and meanwhile, if you've finished your coffee, what do you say to a turn in the Row? I've got my trap here, and a breath of air will freshen us up."

David and Courtney spent the day together, and by evening the young ex- clergyman had made the acquaintance of many of the leading men about town. He had also allowed the fact to transpire that his pecuniary standing was of the soundest kind; but this was done so skillfully-- with such a lofty air--that even Courtney, who was as cynical as any man, was by no means convinced that David's change of fortune had anything to do with his relinquishing the pulpit.

"David Poindexter is no fool," he remarked, confidentially, to a friend. "He has double the stuff in him that the old fellow had. You must get up early to get the better of a man who has been a parson, and seen through himself!"

David, in fact, felt himself the superior, intellectually and by nature, of most of the men he saw. He penetrated and comprehended them, but to them he was impenetrable; a certain air of authority rested upon him; he had abandoned the service of God; but the training whereby he had fitted himself for it stood him in good stead; it had developed his insight, his subtlety, and, strange to say, his powers of dissimulation. Contrary to what is popularly supposed, his study of the affairs of the other world had enabled him to deal with this world's affairs with a half-contemptuous facility. As for the minor technicalities, the social pass-words, and so forth, to which much importance is generally ascribed, David had nothing to fear from them; first, because he was a man of noble manners, naturally as well as by cultivation; and, secondly, because the fact that he had been a clergyman acted as a sort of breastplate against criticism. It would be thought that he chose to appear ignorant of that which he really knew.

As for Mr. Courtney's dinner, though it may doubtless have been a quiet one from his point of view, it differed considerably from such Sunday festivities as David had been accustomed to. A good deal of wine was drunk, and the conversation (a little cautious at first, on David's account) gradually thawed into freedom. It was late when they rose from table; and then a proposition was made to go to a certain well-known club in St. James's Street. David went with the rest, and, for the first time in his life, played cards for money; he lost seven hundred pounds--more money than he had handled during the last three years--but he kept his head, and at three o'clock in the morning drove with Courtney to the latter's lodgings, with five hundred pounds in his pocket over and above the sum with which he had begun to play. Here was a wonderful change in his existence; but it did not seem to him half so wonderful as his reason told him it was. It seemed natural--as if, after much wandering, he had at last found his way into the place where he belonged. It is said that savages, educated from infancy amid civilized surroundings, will, on breathing once more their native air, tear off their clothes and become savages again. Somewhat similar may have been David's case, who, inheriting in a vivid degree the manly instincts of his forefathers, had forcibly and by constraint of circumstances lived a life wholly opposed to these impulses--an artificial life, therefore. But now at length he had come into his birthright, and felt at home.

One episode of the previous evening remained in his memory: it had produced an effect upon him out of proportion with its apparent significance. A gentleman, a guest at the dinner, a small man with sandy hair and keen gray eyes, on being presented to David had looked at him with an expression of shrewd perplexity, and said:

"Have we not met before?"

"It is possible, but I confess I do not recollect it," replied David.

"The name was not Poindexter," continued the other, "but the face-- pardon me--I could have taken my oath to."

"Where did this meeting take place?" asked David, smiling.

"In Paris, at ----'s," said the gray-eyed gentleman (mentioning the name of a well-known French nobleman).

"You are quite certain, of that?"

"Yes. It was but a month since."

"I was never in Paris. For three years I have hardly been out of sight of London," David answered. "What was your friend's name?"

"It has slipped my memory," he replied. "An Italian name, I fancy. But he was a man--pardon me--of very striking appearance, and I conversed with him for more than an hour."

Now it is by no means an uncommon occurrence for two persons to bear a close resemblance to each other, but (aside from the fact that David was anything but an ordinary-looking man) this mistake of his new acquaintance affected him oddly. He involuntarily associated it with the internal and external transformation which had happened to him, and said to himself:

"This counterpart of mine was prophetic: he was what I am to be--what I am." And fantastic though the notion was, he could not rid himself of it.

David returned to Witton about the middle of the week. In the interval he had taken measures to make known to those concerned the revolution of his affairs, and to have the old Lambert mansion opened, and put in some sort of condition for his reception. He had gone forth on foot, an unknown, poor, and humble clergyman; he returned driving behind a pair of horses, by far the most important personage in the town; and yet this outward change was far less great than the change within. His reception could scarcely be called cordial; though not wanting in the technical respect and ceremony due to him as a gentleman of wealth and influence, he could perceive a half concealed suspense and misgiving, due unmistakably to his attitude as a recreant clergyman.

In fact, his worthy parishioners were in a terrible quandary how to reconcile their desire to stand well with their richest fellow- townsman, and their dismayed recognition of that townsman's scandalous professional conduct. David smiled at this, but it made him bitter too. He had intended once more to call the congregation together, and frankly to explain to them the reasons, good or bad, which had induced him to withdraw from active labor in the church. But now he determined to preserve a proud and indifferent silence. There was only one person who had a right to call him to account, and it was not without fearfulness that he looked forward to his meeting with her. However, the sooner such fears are put at rest the better, and he called upon Edith on the evening of his arrival. Her father had been in bed for two days with a cold, and she was sitting alone in the little parlor.

She rose at his entrance with a deep blush, and a look of mixed gladness and anxiety. Her eyes swiftly noted the change in his dress, for he had considerably modified, though not as yet wholly laid aside, the external marks of his profession. She held back from him with a certain strangeness and timidity, so that lie did not kiss her cheek, but only her hand. The first words of greeting were constrained and conventional, but at last he said:

"All is changed, Edith, except our love for each other."

"I do not hold you to that," she answered, quickly.

"But you can not turn me from it," he said, with a smile.

"I do not know you yet," said she, looking away.

"When I last saw you, you said you doubted whether I were my real self. I have become my real self since then."

"Because you are not what you were, it does not follow that you are what you should be."

"Surely, Edith, that is not reasonable. I was what circumstances forced me to be, henceforth I shall be what God made me."

"Did God, then, have no hand in those circumstances?"

"Not more, at all events, than in these."

Edith shook her head. "God does not absolve us from holy vows."

"But how if I can not, with loyalty to my inner conscience, hold to those vows?" exclaimed David, with more warmth. "I have long felt that I was not fitted for this sacred calling. Before the secret tribunal of my self-knowledge, I have stood charged with the sin of hypocrisy. It has been God's will that I be delivered from that sin."

"Why did you not say that before, David?" she demanded, looking at him. "Why did you remain a hypocrite until it was for your worldly benefit to abandon your trust? Can you say, on your word of honor, that you would stand where you do now if you were still poor instead of rich?"

"Men's eyes are to some extent opened and their views are confirmed by events. They make our dreams and forebodings into realities. We question in our minds, and events give us the answers."

"Such an argument might excuse any villainy," said Edith, lifting her head indignantly.

"Villainy! Do you use that word to me?" exclaimed David.

"Not unless your own heart bids me--and I do not know your heart."

"Because you do not love me?"

"You may be right," replied Edith, striving to steady her voice; "but at least I believed I loved you."

"You are cured of that belief, it seems--as I am cured of many foolish faiths," said David, with gloomy bitterness. "Well, so be it! The love that waits upon a fastidious conscience is never the deepest love. My love is not of that complexion. Were it possible that the shadow of sin, or of crime itself, could descend upon you, it would but render you dearer to me than before."

"You may break my heart, David, if you will," cried the girl, tremulously, yet resolutely, "but I reverence love more than I love you."

David had turned away as if to leave the room, but he paused and confronted her once more.

"At any rate, we will understand each other," said he. "Do you make it your condition that I should go back to the ministry?"

Edith was still seated, but the condition of the crisis compelled her to rise. She stood before him, her dark eyes downcast, her lips trembling, nervously drawing the fingers of one hand through the clasp of the other. She was tempted to yield to him, for she could imagine no happiness in life without him; but a rare sanity and integrity of mind made her perceive that he had pushed the matter to a false alternative. It was not a question of preaching or not preaching sermons, but of sinful apostasy from an upright life. At last she raised her eyes, which shone like dark jewels in her pale countenance, and said, slowly, "We had better part."

"Then my sins be upon your head!" cried David, passionately.

The blood mounted to her cheeks at the injustice of this rejoinder, but she either could not or would not answer again. She remained erect and proud until the door had closed between them; what she did after that neither David nor any one else knew.

The apostate David seems to have determined that, if she were to bear the burden of his sins, they should be neither few nor light. His life for many weeks after this interview was a scandal and a disgrace. The old Lambert mansion was the scene of carousals and excesses such as recalled the exploits of the monks of Medmenham. Harwood Courtney, and a score of dissolute gentlemen like him, not to speak of other visitors, thronged the old house day and night; drinking, gaming, and yet wilder doings gave the sober little town no rest, till the Reverend David Poindexter was commonly referred to as the Wicked Parson. Meanwhile Edith Saltine bore herself with a grave, pale impassiveness, which some admired, others wondered at, and others deemed an indication that she had no heart. If she had not, so much the better for her; for her father was almost as difficult to manage as David himself. The old gentleman could neither comprehend nor forgive what seemed to him his daughter's immeasurable perversity. One day she had been all for marrying a poor, unknown preacher; and the next day, when to marry him meant to be the foremost lady in the neighborhood, she dismissed him without appeal. And the worst of it was that, much as the poor colonel's mouth watered at the feasts and festivities of the Lambert mansion, he was prevented by the fatality of his position from taking any part in them. So Edith could find no peace either at home or abroad; and if it dwelt not in her own heart, she was indeed forlorn.

What may have been the cost of all this dissipation it was difficult to say, but several observant persons were of opinion that the parson's income could not long stand it. There were rumors that he had heavy bills owing in several quarters, which he could pay only by realizing some of his investments. On the other hand, it was said that he played high and constantly, and usually had the devil's luck. But it is impossible to gauge the truth of such stories, and the Wicked Parson himself took no pains either to deny or confirm them. He was always the loudest, the gayest, and the most reckless of his company, and the leader and inspirer of all their wild proceedings; but it was noticed that, though he laughed often, he never smiled; and that his face, when in repose, bore traces of anything but happiness. For some cause or other, moreover--but whether maliciously or remorsefully was open to question--he never entirely laid aside his clerical garb; he seemed either to delight in profaning it, or to retain it as the reminder and scourge of his own wickedness.

One night there was a great gathering up at the mansion, and the noise and music were kept up till well past the small hours of the morning. Gradually the guests departed, some going toward London, some elsewhere. At last only Harwood Courtney remained, and he and David sat down in the empty dining-room, disorderly with the remains of the carousal, to play picquet. They played, with short intermissions, for nearly twenty-four hours. At last David threw down his cards, and said, quietly:

"Well, that's all. Give me until to-morrow."

"With all the pleasure in life, my boy," replied the other; "and your revenge, too, if you like. Meanwhile, the best thing we can do is to take a nap."

"You may do so if you please," said David; "for my part, I must take a turn on horseback first. I can never sleep till I have breathed fresh air."

They parted accordingly, Courtney going to his room, and David to the stables, whence he presently issued, mounted on his bay mare, and rode eastward. On his way he passed Colonel Saltine's house, and drew rein for a moment beside it, looking up at Edith's window. It was between four and five o'clock of a morning in early April; the sky was clear, and all was still and peaceful. As he sat in the saddle looking up, the blind of the window was raised and the sash itself opened, and Edith, in her white night-dress, with her heavy brown hair falling round her face and on her shoulders, gazed out. She regarded him with a half- bewildered expression, as if doubting of his reality, For a moment they remained thus; then he waved his hand to her with a wild gesture of farewell, and rode on, passing immediately out of sight behind the dark foliage of the cedar of Lebanon.

On reaching the London high-road the horseman paused once more, and seemed to hesitate what course to pursue; but finally he turned to the right, and rode in a southerly direction. The road wound gently, and dipped and rose to cross low hills; trees bordered the way on each side; and as the sun rose they threw long shadows westward, while the birds warbled and twittered in the fields and hedges. By-and-by a clump of woodland came into view about half a mile off, the road passing through the midst of it. As David entered it at one end, he saw, advancing toward him through the shade and sunlight, a rider mounted on a black horse. The latter seemed to be a very spirited animal, and as David drew near it suddenly shied and reared so violently that any but a practiced horseman would have been unseated. No catastrophe occurred, however, and a moment afterward the two cavaliers were face to face. No sooner had their eyes met than, as if by a common impulse, they both drew rein, and set staring at each other with a curiosity which merged into astonishment. At length the stranger on the black horse gave a short laugh, and said:

"I perceive that the same strange thing has struck us both, sir. If you won't consider it uncivil, I should like to know who you are. My name is Giovanni Lambert."

"Giovanni Lambert," repeated David, with a slight involuntary movement; "unless I am mistaken, I have heard mention of you. But you are not Italian?"

"Only on my mother's side. But you have the advantage of me."

"You will understand that I could not have heard of you without feeling a strong desire to meet you," said David, dismounting as he spoke. "It is, I think, the only desire left me in the world. I had marked this wood, as I came along, as an inviting place to rest in. Would it suit you to spend an hour here, where we can converse better at our ease than in saddle; or does time press you? As for me, I have little more to do with time."

"I am at your service, sir, with pleasure," returned the other, leaping lightly to the ground, and revealing by the movement a pair of small pistols attached to the belt beneath his blue riding surtout. "It was in my mind, also, to stretch my legs and take a pull at my pipe, for, early as it is, I have ridden far this morning."

At the point where they had halted a green lane branched off into the depths of the wood, and down this they passed, leading their horses. When they were out of sight of the road they made their animals fast in such a way that they could crop the grass, and themselves reclined at the foot of a broad-limbed oak, and they remained in converse there for upward of an hour.

In fact, it must been several hours later (for the sun was high in the heavens) when one of them issued from the wood. He was mounted on a black horse, and wore a blue surtout and high boots. After looking up and down the road, and assuring himself that no one was in sight, he turned his horse's head toward London, and set off at a round canter. Coming to a cross-road, he turned to the right, and rode for an hour in that direction, crossing the Thames near Hampton Wick. In the afternoon he entered London from the south, and put up at an obscure hostelry. Having seen his horse attended to, and eaten something himself, he went to bed and slept soundly for eighteen hours. On awaking, he ate heartily again, and spent the rest of the day in writing and arranging a quantity of documents that were packed in his saddle-bags. The next morning early he paid his reckoning, rode across London Bridge, and shaped his course toward the west.

Meanwhile the town of Witton was in vast perturbation. When Mr. Harwood Courtney woke up late in the afternoon, and came yawning down-stairs to get his breakfast, he learned, in answer to his inquiries, that nothing had been seen of David Poindexter since he rode away thirteen hours ago. Mr. Courtney expressed anxiety at this news, and dispatched his own valet and one of David's grooms to make investigations in the neighborhood. These two personages investigated to such good purpose that before night the whole neighborhood was aware that David Poindexter had disappeared. By the next morning it became evident that something had happened to the Wicked Parson, and some people ventured to opine that the thing which had happened to him was that he had run away. And indeed it was astonishing to find to how many worthy people this evil-minded parson was in debt. Every other man you met had a bill against the Reverend David Poindexter in his pocket; and as the day wore on, and still no tidings of the missing man were received, individuals of the sheriff and bailiff species began to be distinguishable amid the crowd. But the great sensation was yet to come. How the report started no one knew, but toward supper-time it passed from mouth to mouth that Mr. Harwood Courtney, in the course of his twenty-four hours of picquet with Poindexter, had won from the latter not his ready money alone, but the entire property and estates that had accrued to him as nearest of kin to the late David Lambert. And it was added that, as the debt was a gambling transaction, and therefore not technically recoverable by process of law, Mr. Courtney was naturally very anxious for his debtor to put in an appearance. Now it so happened that this report, unlike many others ostensibly more plausible, was true in every particular.

Probably there was more gossip at the supper-tables of Witton that night than in any other town of ten times the size in the United Kingdom; and it was formally agreed that Poindexter had escaped to the Continent, and would either remain in hiding there, or take passage by the first opportunity to the American colonies, or the United States, as they had now been called for some years past. Nobody defended the reverend apostate, but, on the other hand, nobody pretended to be sorry for Mr. Harwood Courtney; it was generally agreed that they had both of them got what they deserved. The only question was, What was to become of the property? Some people said it ought to belong to Edith Saltine; but of course poetical justice of that kind was not to be expected.

Edith, meanwhile, had kept herself strictly secluded. She was the last person who had seen David Poindexter, but she had mentioned the fact to no one. She was also the only person who did not believe that he had escaped, but who felt convinced that he was dead, and that he had died by his own hand. That gesture of farewell and of despair which he had made to her as he vanished behind the cedar of Lebanon had for her a significance capable of only one interpretation. Were he alive, he would have returned.

On the evening of the day following the events just recorded, the solitude of her room suddenly became terrible to Edith, and she was irresistibly impelled to dress herself and go forth in the open air. She wound a veil about her head, and, avoiding the main thoroughfare, slipped out of the town unperceived, and gained the free country. After a while she found herself approaching a large tree, which spread its branches across a narrow lane that made a short-cut to the London highway. Beneath the tree was a natural seat, formed of a fragment of stone, and here David and she had often met and sat. It was a mild, still evening; she sat down on the stone, and removed her veil. The moon, then in its first quarter, was low in the west, and shone beneath the branches of the tree.

Presently she was aware--though not by any sound--that some one was approaching, and she drew back in the shadow of the tree. Down the lane came a horseman, mounted on a tall, black horse. The outline of his figure and the manner in which he rode fixed Edith's gaze as if by a spell, and made the blood hum in her ears. Nearer he came, and now his face was discernible in the level moonlight. It was impossible to mistake that countenance: the horseman was David Poindexter. His costume, however, was different from any he had ever before worn; there was nothing clerical about it; nor was that black horse from the Poindexter stables. Then, too, how noiselessly he rode!--as noiselessly as a ghost. That, however, must have been because his horse's hoofs fell on the soft turf. He rode slowly, and his head was bent as if in thought; but almost before Edith could draw her breath, much less to speak, he had passed beneath the boughs of the tree, and was riding on toward the village. Now he had vanished in the vague light and shadow, and a moment later Edith began to doubt whether her senses had not played her a trick. A superstitious horror fell upon her; what she had seen was a spirit, not living flesh and blood. She knelt down by the stone, and remained for a long time with her face hidden upon her arms, and her hands clasped, sometimes praying, sometimes wondering and fearing. At last she rose to her feet, and hastened homeward through the increasing darkness. But before she had reached her house she had discovered that what she had seen was no ghost. The whole village was in a fever of excitement.

Everybody was full of the story. An hour ago who should appear riding quietly up the village street but David Poindexter himself--at least, if it were not he, it was the devil. He seemed to take little notice of the astonished glances that were thrown at him, or, at any rate, not to understand them. Instead of going to the Lambert mansion, he had alighted at the inn, and asked the innkeeper whether he might have lodging there. But when the innkeeper, who had known the reverend gentleman as well as he knew his own sign-board, had addressed him by name, the other had shaken his head, seemed perplexed, and had affirmed that his name was not Poindexter but Lambert; and had added, upon further inquiry, that he was the only son of David Lambert, and was come to claim that gentleman's property, to which he was by law entitled; in proof whereof he had produced various documents, among them the certificates of his mother's marriage and of his own birth.

As to David Poindexter, he declared that he knew not there was such a person; and although no man in his senses could be made to believe that David Poindexter and this so-called Lambert were twain, and not one and the same individual, the latter stoutly maintained his story, and vowed that the truth would sooner or later appear and confirm him. Meanwhile, however, one of his creditors had had him arrested for a debt of eight hundred pounds; and Harwood Courtney had seen him, and said that he was ready to pledge his salvation that the man was Poindexter and nobody else. So here the matter rested for the present. But who ever heard of so strange and audacious an attempt at imposition? The man had not even made any effort to disguise himself further than to put on a different suit of clothes and get another horse; and why, in the name of all that was inconceivable, had he come back to Witton, instead of going to any other part of the earth's surface What could he expect here, except immediate detection, imprisonment, and ruin? Was he insane? He did not seem to be so; but that interpretation of his conduct was not only the most charitable one, but no other could be imagined that would account for the facts.

Witton slept but little that night; but who shall describe its bewilderment when, early in the morning, a constable arrived in the village with the news that the dead body of the Reverend David Poindexter had been found in some woods about fifteen miles off, and that his bay mare had been picked up grazing along the roadside not far from home! Upon the heels of this intelligence came the corpse itself, lying in a country wagon, and the bay mare trotting behind. It was taken out and placed on the table in the inn parlor, where it immediately became the center of a crowd half crazy with curiosity and amazement. The cause of death was found to be the breaking of the vertebral column just at the base of the neck. There was no other injury on the body, and, allowing for the natural changes incident to death, the face was in every particular the face of David Poindexter. The man who called himself Lambert was now brought into the room, and made to stand beside the corpse, which he regarded with a certain calm interest. The resemblance between the two was minute and astonishing; it was found to be impossible, upon that evidence alone, to decide which was David Poindexter.

The matter was brought to trial as promptly as possible. A great number of witnesses identified the prisoner as David Poindexter, but those who had seen the corpse mostly gave their evidence an opposite inclination; and four persons (one of them the gray-eyed gentleman who has been already mentioned) swore positively that the prisoner was Giovanni Lambert, the gray-eyed gentleman adding that he had once met Poindexter, and had confidently taken him to be Lambert.

An attempt was then made to prove that Lambert had murdered Poindexter; but it entirely failed, there being no evidence that the two men had ever so much as met, and there being no conceivable motive for the murder. Lambert, therefore, was permitted to enter undisturbed upon his inheritance; for he had no difficulty in establishing the fact of the elder Lambert's marriage to an Italian woman twenty-three years before. The marriage had been a secret one, and soon after a violent quarrel had taken place between the wife and husband, and they had separated. The following month Giovanni was born prematurely. He had seen his father but once. The quarrel was never made up, but Lambert sent his wife, from time to time, money enough for her support. She had died about ten years ago, and had given her son the papers to establish his identity, telling him that the day would come to use them. Giovanni had been a soldier, fighting against the French in Spain and elsewhere, and had only heard of his father's death a few weeks ago. He had thereupon come to claim his own, with the singular results that we have seen.

Here was the end of the case, so far as the law was concerned; but the real end of it is worth noting. Lambert, by his own voluntary act, paid all the legal debts contracted by Poindexter, and gave Courtney, in settlement of the gambling transaction, a sum of fifty thousand pounds. The remainder of his fortune, which was still considerable, he devoted almost entirely to charitable purposes, doing so much genuine good, in a manner so hearty and unassuming, that he became the object of more personal affection than falls to the lot of most philanthropists. He was of a quiet, sad, and retiring disposition, and uniformly very sparing of words. After a year or so, circumstances brought it about that he and Miss Saltine were associated in some benevolent enterprise, and from that time forward they often consulted together in such matters, Lambert making her the medium of many of his benefactions. Of course the gossips were ready to predict that it would end with a marriage; and indeed it was impossible to see the two together (though both of them, and especially Edith, had altered somewhat with the passage of years) without being reminded of the former love affair in which Lambert's double had been the hero. Did this also occur to Edith? It could hardly have been otherwise, and it would be interesting to speculate on her feelings in the matter; but I have only the story to tell. At all events, they never did marry, though they became very tender friends. At the end of seven years Colonel Saltine died of jaundice; he had been failing in his mind for some time previous, and had always addressed Lambert as Poindexter, and spoken of him as his son-in-law. The year following Lambert himself died, after a brief illness. He left all his property to Edith. She survived to her seventieth year, making it the business of her life to carry out his philanthropic schemes, and she always dressed in widows' weeds. After her death, the following passage was found in one of her private journals. It refers to her last interview with Lambert, on his death- bed:

".... He smiled, and said, 'You will believe, now, that I was sincere in renouncing the ministry, though I have tried to serve the Lord in other ways than from the pulpit.' I felt a shock in my heart, and could hardly say, 'What do you mean, Mr. Lambert?' He replied, 'Surely, Edith, your soul knows, if your reason does not, that I am David Poindexter!' I could not speak. I hid my face in my hands. After a while, in separate sentences, he told me the truth. When he rode forth on that dreadful morning it was with the purpose to die. But he met on the road this Giovanni Lambert, who so marvelously resembled him, and they sat down together in the wood and talked, and Giovanni told him all the story of his life.... As Giovanni was about to mount his horse, which was very restive, he saw a violet in the grass, and stooped to pick it. The horse lashed out with its heels, and struck him in the back of the neck and killed him.... Then the idea came to David to exchange clothes with the dead man, and to take his papers, and personate him. Thus, he could escape from the individuality which was his curse, and find his true self, as it were, in another person. He said, too, that his greatest hope had been to win my love and make me his wife; but he found that he could not bring himself to attempt that, unless he confessed his falsehood to me, and he had feared that this confession would turn me from him forever. I wept, and told him that my heart had been his almost from the first, because I always thought of him as David, and that I would have loved him through all things. He said, 'Then God has been more merciful to me than I deserve; but, doubtless, it is also of His mercy that we have remained unmarried.' But I was in an agony, and could not yet be reconciled. At last he said, 'Will you kiss me, Edith?' and afterward he said, 'My wife!' and that was his last word. But we shall meet again!"

KEN'S MYSTERY.

One cool October evening--it was the last day of the month, and unusually cool for the time of year--I made up my mind to go and spend an hour or two with my friend Keningale. Keningale was an artist (as well as a musical amateur and poet), and had a very delightful studio built onto his house, in which he was wont to sit of an evening. The studio had a cavernous fire-place, designed in imitation of the old- fashioned fire-places of Elizabethan manor-houses, and in it, when the temperature out-doors warranted, he would build up a cheerful fire of dry logs. It would suit me particularly well, I thought, to go and have a quiet pipe and chat in front of that fire with my friend.

I had not had such a chat for a very long time--not, in fact, since Keningale (or Ken, as his friends called him) had returned from his visit to Europe the year before. He went abroad, as he affirmed at the time, "for purposes of study," whereat we all smiled, for Ken, so far as we knew him, was more likely to do anything else than to study. He was a young fellow of buoyant temperament, lively and social in his habits, of a brilliant and versatile mind, and possessing an income of twelve or fifteen thousand dollars a year; he could sing, play, scribble, and paint very cleverly, and some of his heads and figure- pieces were really well done, considering that he never had any regular training in art; but he was not a worker. Personally he was fine- looking, of good height and figure, active, healthy, and with a remarkably fine brow, and clear, full-gazing eye. Nobody was surprised at his going to Europe, no-body expected him to do anything there except amuse himself, and few anticipated that he would be soon again seen in New York. He was one of the sort that find Europe agree with them. Off he went, therefore; and in the course of a few months the rumor reached us that he was engaged to a handsome and wealthy New York girl whom he had met in London. This was nearly all we did hear of him until, not very long afterward, he turned up again on Fifth Avenue, to every one's astonishment; made no satisfactory answer to those who wanted to know how he happened to tire so soon of the Old World; while, as to the reported engagement, he cut short all allusion to that in so peremptory a manner as to show that it was not a permissible topic of conversation with him. It was surmised that the lady had jilted him; but, on the other hand, she herself returned home not a great while after, and, though she had plenty of opportunities, she has never married to this day.

Be the rights of that matter what they may, it was soon remarked that Ken was no longer the careless and merry fellow he used to be; on the contrary, he appeared grave, moody, averse from general society, and habitually taciturn and undemonstrative even in the company of his most intimate friends. Evidently something had happened to him, or he had done something. What? Had he committed a murder? or joined the Nihilists? or was his unsuccessful love affair at the bottom of it? Some declared that the cloud was only temporary, and would soon pass away. Nevertheless, up to the period of which I am writing, it had not passed away, but had rather gathered additional gloom, and threatened to become permanent.

Meanwhile I had met him twice or thrice at the club, at the opera, or in the street, but had as yet had no opportunity of regularly renewing my acquaintance with him. We had been on a footing of more than common intimacy in the old days, and I was not disposed to think that he would refuse to renew the former relations now. But what I had heard and myself seen of his changed condition imparted a stimulating tinge of suspense or curiosity to the pleasure with which I looked forward to the prospects of this evening. His house stood at a distance of two or three miles beyond the general range of habitations in New York at this time, and as I walked briskly along in the clear twilight air I had leisure to go over in my mind all that I had known of Ken and had divined of his character. After all, had there not always been something in his nature--deep down, and held in abeyance by the activity of his animal spirits--but something strange and separate, and capable of developing under suitable conditions into--into what? As I asked myself this question I arrived at his door; and it was with a feeling of relief that I felt the next moment the cordial grasp of his hand, and his voice bidding me welcome in a tone that indicated unaffected gratification at my presence. He drew me at once into the studio, relieved me of my hat and cane, and then put his hand on my shoulder.

"I am glad to see you," he repeated, with singular earnestness--"glad to see you and to feel you; and to-night of all nights in the year."

"Why to-night especially?"

"Oh, never mind. It's just as well, too, you didn't let me know beforehand you were coming; the unreadiness is all, to paraphrase the poet. Now, with you to help me, I can drink a glass of whisky and water and take a bit draw of the pipe. This would have been a grim night for me if I'd been left to myself."

"In such a lap of luxury as this, too!" said I, looking round at the glowing fire-place, the low, luxurious chairs, and all the rich and sumptuous fittings of the room. "I should have thought a condemned murderer might make himself comfortable here."

"Perhaps; but that's not exactly my category at present. But have you forgotten what night this is? This is November-eve, when, as tradition asserts, the dead arise and walk about, and fairies, goblins, and spiritual beings of all kinds have more freedom and power than on any other day of the year. One can see you've never been in Ireland."

"I wasn't aware till now that you had been there, either."

"Yes, I have been in Ireland. Yes--" He paused, sighed, and fell into a reverie, from which, however, he soon roused himself by an effort, and went to a cabinet in a corner of the room for the liquor and tobacco. While he was thus employed I sauntered about the studio, taking note of the various beauties, grotesquenesses, and curiosities that it contained. Many things were there to repay study and arouse admiration; for Ken was a good collector, having excellent taste as well as means to back it. But, upon the whole, nothing interested me more than some studies of a female head, roughly done in oils, and, judging from the sequestered positions in which I found them, not intended by the artist for exhibition or criticism. There were three or four of these studies, all of the same face, but in different poses and costumes. In one the head was enveloped in a dark hood, overshadowing and partly concealing the features; in another she seemed to be peering duskily through a latticed casement, lit by a faint moonlight; a third showed her splendidly attired in evening costume, with jewels in her hair and cars, and sparkling on her snowy bosom. The expressions were as various as the poses; now it was demure penetration, now a subtle inviting glance, now burning passion, and again a look of elfish and elusive mockery. In whatever phase, the countenance possessed a singular and poignant fascination, not of beauty merely, though that was very striking, but of character and quality likewise.

"Did you find this model abroad?" I inquired at length. "She has evidently inspired yon, and I don't wonder at it."

Ken, who had been mixing the punch, and had not noticed my movements, now looked up, and said: "I didn't mean those to be seen. They don't satisfy me, and I am going to destroy them; but I couldn't rest till I'd made some attempts to reproduce--What was it you asked? Abroad? Yes--or no. They were all painted here within the last six weeks."

"'Whether they satisfy you or not, they are by far the best things of yours I have ever seen."

"'Well, let them alone, and tell me what you think of this beverage. To my thinking, it goes to the right spot. It owes its existence to your coming here. I can't drink alone, and those portraits are not company, though, for aught I know, she might have come out of the canvas to- night and sat down in that chair." Then, seeing my inquiring look, he added, with a hasty laugh, "It's November-eve, you know, when anything may happen, provided its strange enough. Well, here's to ourselves."

We each swallowed a deep draught of the smoking and aromatic liquor, and set down our glasses with approval. The punch was excellent. Ken now opened a box of cigars, and we seated ourselves before the fire- place.

"All we need now," I remarked, after a short silence, "is a little music. By-the-by, Ken, have you still got the banjo I gave you before you went abroad?"

He paused so long before replying that I supposed he had not heard my question. "I have got it," he said, at length, "but it will never make any more music."

"Got broken, eh? Can't it be mended? It was a fine instrument."

"It's not broken, but it's past mending. You shall see for yourself."

He arose as he spoke, and going to another part of the studio, opened a black oak coffer, and took out of it a long object wrapped up in a piece of faded yellow silk. He handed it to me, and when I had unwrapped it, there appeared a thing that might once have been a banjo, but had little resemblance to one now. It bore every sign of extreme age. The wood of the handle was honeycombed with the gnawings of worms, and dusty with dry-rot. The parchment head was green with mold, and hung in shriveled tatters. The hoop, which was of solid silver, was so blackened and tarnished that it looked like dilapidated iron. The strings were gone, and most of the tuning-screws had dropped out of their decayed sockets. Altogether it had the appearance of having been made before the Flood, and been forgotten in the forecastle of Noah's Ark ever since.

"It is a curious relic, certainly," I said. "Where did you come across it? I had no idea that the banjo was invented so long ago as this. It certainly can't be less than two hundred years old, and may be much older than that."

Ken smiled gloomily. "You are quite right," lie said; "it is at least two hundred years old, and yet it is the very same banjo that you gave me a year ago."

"Hardly," I returned, smiling in my turn, "since that was made to my order with a view to presenting it to you."

"I know that; but the two hundred years have passed since then. Yes; it is absurd and impossible, I know, but nothing is truer. That banjo, which was made last year, existed in the sixteenth century, and has been rotting ever since. Stay. Give it to me a moment, and I'll convince you. You recollect that your name and mine, with the date, were engraved on the silver hoop?"

"Yes; and there was a private mark of my own there, also."

"Very well," said Ken, who had been rubbing a place on the hoop with a corner of the yellow silk wrapper; "look at that."

I took the decrepit instrument from him, and examined the spot which he had rubbed. It was incredible, sure enough; but there were the names and the date precisely as I had caused them to be engraved; and there, moreover, was my own private mark, which I had idly made with an old etching point not more than eighteen months before. After convincing myself that there was no mistake, I laid the banjo across my knees, and stared at my friend in bewilderment. He sat smoking with a kind of grim composure, his eyes fixed upon the blazing logs.

"I'm mystified, I confess," said I. "Come; what is the joke? What method have you discovered of producing the decay of centuries on this unfortunate banjo in a few months? And why did you do it? I have heard of an elixir to counteract the effects of time, but your recipe seems to work the other way--to make time rush forward at two hundred times his usual rate, in one place, while he jogs on at his usual gait elsewhere. Unfold your mystery, magician. Seriously, Ken, how on earth did the thing happen?"

"I know no more about it than you do," was his reply. "Either you and I and all the rest of the living world are insane, or else there has been wrought a miracle as strange as any in tradition. How can I explain it? It is a common saying--a common experience, if you will--that we may, on certain trying or tremendous occasions, live years in one moment. But that's a mental experience, not a physical one, and one that applies, at all events, only to human beings, not to senseless things of wood and metal. You imagine the thing is some trick or jugglery. If it be, I don't know the secret of it. There's no chemical appliance that I ever heard of that will get a piece of solid wood into that condition in a few months, or a few years. And it wasn't done in a few years, or a few months either. A year ago today at this very hour that banjo was as sound as when it left the maker's hands, and twenty-four hours afterward--I'm telling you the simple truth--it was as you see it now."

The gravity and earnestness with which Ken made this astounding statement were evidently not assumed, He believed every word that he uttered. I knew not what to think. Of course my friend might be insane, though he betrayed none of the ordinary symptoms of mania; but, however that might be, there was the banjo, a witness whose silent testimony there was no gainsaying. The more I meditated on the matter the more inconceivable did it appear. Two hundred years--twenty-four hours; these were the terms of the proposed equation. Ken and the banjo both affirmed that the equation had been made; all worldly knowledge and experience affirmed it to be impossible. "What was the explanation? What is time? What is life? I felt myself beginning to doubt the reality of all things. And so this was the mystery which my friend had been brooding over since his return from abroad. No wonder it had changed him. More to be wondered at was it that it had not changed him more.

"Can you tell me the whole story?" I demanded at length.

Ken quaffed another draught from his glass of whisky and water and rubbed his hand through his thick brown beard. "I have never spoken to any one of it heretofore," he said, "and I had never meant to speak of it. But I'll try and give you some idea of what it was. You know me better than any one else; you'll understand the thing as far as it can ever be understood, and perhaps I may be relieved of some of the oppression it has caused me. For it is rather a ghastly memory to grapple with alone, I can tell you."

Hereupon, without further preface, Ken related the following tale. He was, I may observe in passing, a naturally fine narrator. There were deep, lingering tones in his voice, and he could strikingly enhance the comic or pathetic effect of a sentence by dwelling here and there upon some syllable. His features were equally susceptible of humorous and of solemn expressions, and his eyes were in form and hue wonderfully adapted to showing great varieties of emotion. Their mournful aspect was extremely earnest and affecting; and when Ken was giving utterance to some mysterious passage of the tale they had a doubtful, melancholy, exploring look which appealed irresistibly to the imagination. But the interest of his story was too pressing to allow of noticing these incidental embellishments at the time, though they doubtless had their influence upon me all the same.

"I left New York on an Inman Line steamer, you remember," began Ken, "and landed at Havre. I went the usual round of sight-seeing on the Continent, and got round to London in July, at the height of the season. I had good introductions, and met any number of agreeable and famous people. Among others was a young lady, a countrywoman of my own --you know whom I mean--who interested me very much, and before her family left London she and I were engaged. We parted there for the time, because she had the Continental trip still to make, while I wanted to take the opportunity to visit the north of England and Ireland. I landed at Dublin about the 1st of October, and, zigzagging about the country, I found myself in County Cork about two weeks later.

"There is in that region some of the most lovely scenery that human eyes ever rested on, and it seems to be less known to tourists than many places of infinitely less picturesque value. A lonely region too: during my rambles I met not a single stranger like myself, and few enough natives. It seems incredible that so beautiful a country should be so deserted. After walking a dozen Irish miles you come across a group of two or three one-roomed cottages, and, like as not, one or more of those will have the roof off and the walls in ruins. The few peasants whom one sees, however, are affable and hospitable, especially when they hear you are from that terrestrial heaven whither most of their friends and relatives have gone before them. They seem simple and primitive enough at first sight, and yet they are as strange and incomprehensible a race as any in the world. They are as superstitious, as credulous of marvels, fairies, magicians, and omens, as the men whom St. Patrick preached to, and at the same time they are shrewd, skeptical, sensible, and bottomless liars.

Upon the whole, I met with no nation on my travels whose company I enjoyed so much, or who inspired me with so much kindliness, curiosity, and repugnance.

"At length I got to a place on the sea-coast, which I will not further specify than to say that it is not many miles from Ballymacheen, on the south shore. I have seen Venice and Naples, I have driven along the Cornice Road, I have spent a month at our own Mount Desert, and I say that all of them together are not so beautiful as this glowing, deep- hued, soft-gleaming, silvery-lighted, ancient harbor and town, with the tall hills crowding round it and the black cliffs and headlands planting their iron feet in the blue, transparent sea. It is a very old place, and has had a history which it has outlived ages since. It may once have had two or three thousand inhabitants; it has scarce five or six hundred to day. Half the houses are in ruins or have disappeared; many of the remainder are standing empty. All the people are poor, most of them abjectly so; they saunter about with bare feet and uncovered heads, the women in quaint black or dark-blue cloaks, the men in such anomalous attire as only an Irishman knows how to get together, the children half naked. The only comfortable-looking people are the monks and the priests, and the soldiers in the fort. For there is a fort there, constructed on the huge ruins of one which may have done duty in the reign of Edward the Black Prince, or earlier, in whose mossy embrasures are mounted a couple of cannon, which occasionally sent a practice-shot or two at the cliff on the other side of the harbor. The garrison consists of a dozen men and three or four officers and non- commissioned officers. I suppose they are relieved occasionally, but those I saw seemed to have become component parts of their surroundings.

"I put up at a wonderful little old inn, the only one in the place, and took my meals in a dining-saloon fifteen feet by nine, with a portrait of George I (a print varnished to preserve it) hanging over the mantel- piece. On the second evening after dinner a young gentleman came in-- the dining-saloon being public property of course--and ordered some bread and cheese and a bottle of Dublin stout. We presently fell into talk; he turned out to be an officer from the fort, Lieutenant O'Connor, and a fine young specimen of the Irish soldier he was. After telling me all he knew about the town, the surrounding country, his friends, and himself, he intimated a readiness to sympathize with whatever tale I might choose to pour into his ear; and I had pleasure in trying to rival his own outspokenness. We became excellent friends; we had up a half-pint of Kinahan's whisky, and the lieutenant expressed himself in terms of high praise of my countrymen, my country, and my own particular cigars. When it became time for him to depart I accompanied him--for there was a splendid moon abroad--and bade him farewell at the fort entrance, having promised to come over the next day and make the acquaintance of the other fellows. 'And mind your eye, now, going back, my dear boy,' he called out, as I turned my face homeward. 'Faith, 'tis a spooky place, that graveyard, and you'll as likely meet the black woman there as anywhere else!'

"The graveyard was a forlorn and barren spot on the hill-side, just the hither side of the fort: thirty or forty rough head-stones, few of which retained any semblance of the perpendicular, while many were so shattered and decayed as to seem nothing more than irregular natural projections from the ground. Who the black woman might be I knew not, and did not stay to inquire. I had never been subject to ghostly apprehensions, and as a matter of fact, though the path I had to follow was in places very bad going, not to mention a hap-hazard scramble over a ruined bridge that covered a deep-lying brook, I reached my inn without any adventure whatever.

"The next day I kept my appointment at the fort, and found no reason to regret it; and my friendly sentiments were abundantly reciprocated, thanks more especially, perhaps, to the success of my banjo, which I carried with me, and which was as novel as it was popular with those who listened to it. The chief personages in the social circle besides my friend the lieutenant were Major Molloy, who was in command, a racy and juicy old campaigner, with a face like a sunset, and the surgeon, Dr. Dudeen, a long, dry, humorous genius, with a wealth of anecdotical and traditional lore at his command that I have never seen surpassed. We had a jolly time of it, and it was the precursor of many more like it. The remains of October slipped away rapidly, and I was obliged to remember that I was a traveler in Europe, and not a resident in Ireland. The major, the surgeon, and the lieutenant all protested cordially against my proposed departure, but, as there was no help for it, they arranged a farewell dinner to take place in the fort on All- halloween.

"I wish you could have been at that dinner with me! It was the essence of Irish good-fellowship. Dr. Dudeen was in great force; the major was better than the best of Lever's novels; the lieutenant was overflowing with hearty good-humor, merry chaff, and sentimental rhapsodies anent this or the other pretty girl of the neighborhood. For my part I made the banjo ring as it had never rung before, and the others joined in the chorus with a mellow strength of lungs such as you don't often hear outside of Ireland. Among the stories that Dr. Dudeen regaled us with was one about the Kern of Querin and his wife, Ethelind Fionguala-- which being interpreted signifies 'the white-shouldered.' The lady, it appears, was originally betrothed to one O'Connor (here the lieutenant smacked his lips), but was stolen away on the wedding night by a party of vampires, who, it would seem, were at that period a prominent feature among the troubles of Ireland. But as they were bearing her along--she being unconscious--to that supper where she was not to eat but to be eaten, the young Kern of Querin, who happened to be out duck- shooting, met the party, and emptied his gun at it. The vampires fled, and the Kern carried the fair lady, still in a state of insensibility, to his house. 'And by the same token, Mr. Keningale,' observed the doctor, knocking the ashes out of his pipe, 'ye're after passing that very house on your way here. The one with the dark archway underneath it, and the big mullioned window at the corner, ye recollect, hanging over the street as I might say--'

"'Go 'long wid the house, Dr. Dudeen, dear,' interrupted the lieutenant; 'sure can't you see we're all dying to know what happened to sweet Miss Fionguala, God be good to her, when I was after getting her safe up-stairs--'

"'Faith, then, I can tell ye that myself, Mr. O'Connor,' exclaimed the major, imparting a rotary motion to the remnants of whisky in his tumbler. ''Tis a question to be solved on general principles, as Colonel O'Halloran said that time he was asked what he'd do if he'd been the Book o' Wellington, and the Prussians hadn't come up in the nick o' time at Waterloo. 'Faith,' says the colonel, 'I'll tell ye--'

"'Arrah, then, major, why would ye be interruptin' the doctor, and Mr. Keningale there lettin' his glass stay empty till he hears--The Lord save us! the bottle's empty!'

"In the excitement consequent upon this discovery, the thread of the doctor's story was lost; and before it could be recovered the evening had advanced so far that I felt obliged to withdraw. It took some time to make my proposition heard and comprehended; and a still longer time to put it in execution; so that it was fully midnight before I found myself standing in the cool pure air outside the fort, with the farewells of my boon companions ringing in my ears.

"Considering that it had been rather a wet evening in-doors, I was in a remarkably good state of preservation, and I therefore ascribed it rather to the roughness of the road than to the smoothness of the liquor, when, after advancing a few rods, I stumbled and fell. As I picked myself up I fancied I had heard a laugh, and supposed that the lieutenant, who had accompanied me to the gate, was making merry over my mishap; but on looking round I saw that the gate was closed and no one was visible. The laugh, moreover, had seemed to be close at hand, and to be even pitched in a key that was rather feminine than masculine. Of course I must have been deceived; nobody was near me: my imagination had played me a trick, or else there was more truth than poetry in the tradition that Halloween is the carnival-time of disembodied spirits. It did not occur to me at the time that a stumble is held by the superstitious Irish to be an evil omen, and had I remembered it it would only have been to laugh at it. At all events, I was physically none the worse for my fall, and I resumed my way immediately.

"But the path was singularly difficult to find, or rather the path I was following did not seem to be the right one. I did not recognize it; I could have sworn (except I knew the contrary) that I had never seen it before. The moon had risen, though her light was as yet obscured by clouds, but neither my immediate surroundings nor the general aspect of the region appeared familiar. Dark, silent hill-sides mounted up on either hand, and the road, for the most part, plunged downward, as if to conduct me into the bowels of the earth. The place was alive with strange echoes, so that at times I seemed to be walking through the midst of muttering voices and mysterious whispers, and a wild, faint sound of laughter seemed ever and anon to reverberate among the passes of the hills. Currents of colder air sighing up through narrow defiles and dark crevices touched my face as with airy fingers. A certain feeling of anxiety and insecurity began to take possession of me, though there was no definable cause for it, unless that I might be belated in getting home. With the perverse instinct of those who are lost I hastened my steps, but was impelled now and then to glance back over my shoulder, with a sensation of being pursued. But no living creature was in sight. The moon, however, had now risen higher, and the clouds that were drifting slowly across the sky flung into the naked valley dusky shadows, which occasionally assumed shapes that looked like the vague semblance of gigantic human forms.

"How long I had been hurrying onward I know not, when, with a kind of suddenness, I found myself approaching a graveyard. It was situated on the spur of a hill, and there was no fence around it, nor anything to protect it from the incursions of passers-by. There was something in the general appearance of this spot that made me half fancy I had seen it before; and I should have taken it to be the same that I had often noticed on my way to the fort, but that the latter was only a few hundred yards distant therefrom, whereas I must have traversed several miles at least. As I drew near, moreover, I observed that the head- stones did not appear so ancient and decayed as those of the other. But what chiefly attracted my attention was the figure that was leaning or half sitting upon one of the largest of the upright slabs near the road. It was a female figure draped in black, and a closer inspection-- for I was soon within a few yards of her--showed that she wore the calla, or long hooded cloak, the most common as well as the most ancient garment of Irish women, and doubtless of Spanish origin.

"I was a trifle startled by this apparition, so unexpected as it was, and so strange did it seem that any human creature should be at that hour of the night in so desolate and sinister a place. Involuntarily I paused as I came opposite her, and gazed at her intently. But the moonlight fell behind her, and the deep hood of her cloak so completely shadowed her face that I was unable to discern anything but the sparkle of a pair of eyes, which appeared to be returning my gaze with much vivacity.

"'You seem to be at home here,' I said, at length. 'Can you tell me where I am?'

"Hereupon the mysterious personage broke into a light laugh, which, though in itself musical and agreeable, was of a timbre and intonation that caused my heart to beat rather faster than my late pedestrian exertions warranted; for it was the identical laugh (or so my imagination persuaded me) that had echoed in my ears as I arose from my tumble an hour or two ago. For the rest, it was the laugh of a young woman, and presumably of a pretty one; and yet it had a wild, airy, mocking quality, that seemed hardly human at all, or not, at any rate, characteristic of a being of affections and limitations like unto ours. But this impression of mine was fostered, no doubt, by the unusual and uncanny circumstances of the occasion.

"'Sure, sir,' said she, 'you're at the grave of Ethelind Fionguala.'

"As she spoke she rose to her feet, and pointed to the inscription on the stone. I bent forward, and was able, without much difficulty, to decipher the name, and a date which indicated that the occupant of the grave must have entered the disembodied state between two and three centuries ago.

"'And who are you?' was my next question.

"'I'm called Elsie,' she replied. 'But where would your honor be going November-eve?'

"I mentioned my destination, and asked her whether she could direct me thither.

"'Indeed, then, 'tis there I'm going myself,' Elsie replied; 'and if your honor'll follow me, and play me a tune on the pretty instrument, 'tisn't long we'll be on the road.'

"She pointed to the banjo which I carried wrapped up under my arm. How she knew that it was a musical instrument I could not imagine; possibly, I thought, she may have seen me playing on it as I strolled about the environs of the town. Be that as it may, I offered no opposition to the bargain, and further intimated that I would reward her more substantially on our arrival. At that she laughed again, and made a peculiar gesture with her hand above her head. I uncovered my banjo, swept my fingers across the strings, and struck into a fantastic dance-measure, to the music of which we proceeded along the path, Elsie slightly in advance, her feet keeping time to the airy measure. In fact, she trod so lightly, with an elastic, undulating movement, that with a little more it seemed as if she might float onward like a spirit. The extreme whiteness of her feet attracted my eye, and I was surprised to find that instead of being bare, as I had supposed, these were incased in white satin slippers quaintly embroidered with gold thread.

"'Elsie,' said I, lengthening my steps so as to come up with her, 'where do you live, and what do you do for a living?'

"'Sure, I live by myself,' she answered; 'and if you'd be after knowing how, you must come and see for yourself.'

"'Are you in the habit of walking over the hills at night in shoes like that?'

"'And why would I not?' she asked, in her turn. 'And where did your honor get the pretty gold ring on your finger?'

"The ring, which was of no great intrinsic value, had struck my eye in an old curiosity-shop in Cork. It was an antique of very old-fashioned design, and might have belonged (as the vender assured me was the case) to one of the early kings or queens of Ireland.

"'Do you like it?' said I.

"'Will your honor be after making a present of it to Elsie?' she returned, with an insinuating tone and turn of the head.

"'Maybe I will, Elsie, on one condition. I am an artist; I make pictures of people. If you will promise to come to my studio and let me paint your portrait, I'll give you the ring, and some money besides.'

"'And will you give me the ring now?' said Elsie.

"'Yes, if you'll promise.'

"'And will you play the music to me?' she continued.

"'As much as you like.'

"'But maybe I'll not be handsome enough for ye,' said she, with a glance of her eyes beneath the dark hood.

"'I'll take the risk of that,' I answered, laughing, 'though, all the same, I don't mind taking a peep beforehand to remember you by.' So saying, I put forth a hand to draw back the concealing hood. But Elsie eluded me, I scarce know how, and laughed a third time, with the same airy, mocking cadence.

"'Give me the ring first, and then you shall see me,' she said, coaxingly.

"'Stretch out your hand, then,' returned I, removing the ring from my finger. 'When we are better acquainted, Elsie, you won't be so suspicious.'

"She held out a slender, delicate hand, on the forefinger of which I slipped the ring. As I did so, the folds of her cloak fell a little apart, affording me a glimpse of a white shoulder and of a dress that seemed in that deceptive semi-darkness to be wrought of rich and costly material; and I caught, too, or so I fancied, the frosty sparkle of precious stones.

"'Arrah, mind where ye tread!' said Elsie, in a sudden, sharp tone.

"I looked round, and became aware for the first time that we were standing near the middle of a ruined bridge which spanned a rapid stream that flowed at a considerable depth below. The parapet of the bridge on one side was broken down, and I must have been, in fact, in imminent danger of stepping over into empty air. I made my way cautiously across the decaying structure; but, when I turned to assist

Elsie, she was nowhere to be seen.

"What had become of the girl? I called, but no answer came. I gazed about on every side, but no trace of her was visible. Unless she had plunged into the narrow abyss at my feet, there was no place where she could have concealed herself--none at least that I could discover. She had vanished, nevertheless; and since her disappearance must have been premeditated, I finally came to the conclusion that it was useless to attempt to find her. She would present herself again in her own good time, or not at all. She had given me the slip very cleverly, and I must make the best of it. The adventure was perhaps worth the ring.

"On resuming my way, I was not a little relieved to find that I once more knew where I was. The bridge that I had just crossed was none other than the one I mentioned some time back; I was within a mile of the town, and my way lay clear before me. The moon, moreover, had now quite dispersed the clouds, and shone down with exquisite brilliance. Whatever her other failings, Elsie had been a trustworthy guide; she had brought me out of the depth of elf-land into the material world again. It had been a singular adventure, certainly; and I mused over it with a sense of mysterious pleasure as I sauntered along, humming snatches of airs, and accompanying myself on the strings. Hark! what light step was that behind me? It sounded like Elsie's; but no, Elsie was not there. The same impression or hallucination, however, recurred several times before I reached the outskirts of the town--the tread of an airy foot behind or beside my own. The fancy did not make me nervous; on the contrary, I was pleased with the notion of being thus haunted, and gave myself up to a romantic and genial vein of reverie.

"After passing one or two roofless and moss-grown cottages, I entered the narrow and rambling street which leads through the town. This street a short distance down widens a little, as if to afford the wayfarer space to observe a remarkable old house that stands on the northern side. The house was built of stone, and in a noble style of architecture; it reminded me somewhat of certain palaces of the old Italian nobility that I had seen on the Continent, and it may very probably have been built by one of the Italian or Spanish immigrants of the sixteenth or seventeenth century. The molding of the projecting windows and arched doorway was richly carved, and upon the front of the building was an escutcheon wrought in high relief, though I could not make out the purport of the device. The moonlight falling upon this picturesque pile enhanced all its beauties, and at the same time made it seem like a vision that might dissolve away when the light ceased to shine. I must often have seen the house before, and yet I retained no definite recollection of it; I had never until now examined it with my eyes open, so to speak. Leaning against the wall on the opposite side of the street, I contemplated it for a long while at my leisure. The window at the corner was really a very fine and massive affair. It projected over the pavement below, throwing a heavy shadow aslant; the frames of the diamond-paned lattices were heavily mullioned. How often in past ages had that lattice been pushed open by some fair hand, revealing to a lover waiting beneath in the moonlight the charming countenance of his high-born mistress! Those were brave days. They had passed away long since. The great house had stood empty for who could tell how many years; only bats and vermin were its inhabitants. Where now were those who had built it? and who were they? Probably the very name of them was forgotten.

"As I continued to stare upward, however, a conjecture presented itself to my mind which rapidly ripened into a conviction. Was not this the house that Dr. Dudeen had described that very evening as having been formerly the abode of the Kern of Querin and his mysterious bride? There was the projecting window, the arched doorway. Yes, beyond a doubt this was the very house. I emitted a low exclamation of renewed interest and pleasure, and my speculations took a still more imaginative, but also a more definite turn.

"What had been the fate of that lovely lady after the Kern had brought her home insensible in his arms? Did she recover, and were they married and made happy ever after; or had the sequel been a tragic one? I remembered to have read that the victims of vampires generally became vampires themselves. Then my thoughts went back to that grave on the hill-side. Surely that was unconsecrated ground. Why had they buried her there? Ethelind of the white shoulder! Ah! why had not I lived in those days; or why might not some magic cause them to live again for me? Then would I seek this street at midnight, and standing here beneath her window, I would lightly touch the strings of my bandore until the casement opened cautiously and she looked down. A sweet vision indeed! And what prevented my realizing it? Only a matter of a couple of centuries or so. And was time, then, at which poets and philosophers sneer, so rigid and real a matter that a little faith and imagination might not overcome it? At all events, I had my banjo, the bandore's legitimate and lineal descendant, and the memory of Fionguala should have the love-ditty.

"Hereupon, having retuned the instrument, I launched forth into an old Spanish love-song, which I had met with in some moldy library during my travels, and had set to music of my own. I sang low, for the deserted street re-echoed the lightest sound, and what I sang must reach only my lady's ears. The words were warm with the fire of the ancient Spanish chivalry, and I threw into their expression all the passion of the lovers of romance. Surely Fionguala, the white-shouldered, would hear, and awaken from her sleep of centuries, and come to the latticed casement and look down! Hist! see yonder! What light--what shadow is that that seems to flit from room to room within the abandoned house, and now approaches the mullioned window? Are my eyes dazzled by the play of the moonlight, or does the casement move--does it open? Nay, this is no delusion; there is no error of the senses here. There is simply a woman, young, beautiful, and richly attired, bending forward from the window, and silently beckoning me to approach.

"Too much amazed to be conscious of amazement, I advanced until I stood directly beneath the casement, and the lady's face, as she stooped toward me, was not more than twice a man's height from my own. She smiled and kissed her finger-tips; something white fluttered in her hand, then fell through the air to the ground at my feet. The next moment she had withdrawn, and I heard the lattice close. I picked up what she had let fall; it was a delicate lace handkerchief, tied to the handle of an elaborately wrought bronze key. It was evidently the key of the house, and invited me to enter. I loosened it from the handkerchief, which bore a faint, delicious perfume, like the aroma of flowers in an ancient garden, and turned to the arched doorway. I felt no misgiving, and scarcely any sense of strangeness. All was as I had wished it to be, and as it should be; the mediaeval age was alive once more, and as for myself, I almost felt the velvet cloak hanging from my shoulder and the long rapier dangling at my belt. Standing in front of the door I thrust the key into the lock, turned it, and felt the bolt yield. The next instant the door was opened, apparently from within; I stepped across the threshold, the door closed again, and I was alone in the house, and in darkness.

"Not alone, however! As I extended my hand to grope my way it was met by another hand, soft, slender, and cold, which insinuated itself gently into mine and drew me forward. Forward I went, nothing loath; the darkness was impenetrable, but I could hear the light rustle of a dress close to me, and the same delicious perfume that had emanated from the handkerchief enriched the air that I breathed, while the little hand that clasped and was clasped by my own alternately tightened and half relaxed the hold of its soft cold fingers. In this manner, and treading lightly, we traversed what I presumed to be a long, irregular passageway, and ascended a staircase. Then another corridor, until finally we paused, a door opened, emitting a flood of soft light, into which we entered, still hand in hand. The darkness and the doubt were at an end.

"The room was of imposing dimensions, and was furnished and decorated in a style of antique splendor. The walls were draped with mellow hues of tapestry; clusters of candles burned in polished silver sconces, and were reflected and multiplied in tall mirrors placed in the four corners of the room. The heavy beams of the dark oaken ceiling crossed each other in squares, and were laboriously carved; the curtains and the drapery of the chairs were of heavy-figured damask. At one end of the room was a broad ottoman, and in front of it a table, on which was set forth, in massive silver dishes, a sumptuous repast, with wines in crystal beakers. At the side was a vast and deep fire-place, with space enough on the broad hearth to burn whole trunks of trees. No fire, however, was there, but only a great heap of dead embers; and the room, for all its magnificence, was cold--cold as a tomb, or as my lady's hand--and it sent a subtle chill creeping to my heart.

"But my lady! how fair she was! I gave but a passing glance at the room; my eyes and my thoughts were all for her. She was dressed in white, like a bride; diamonds sparkled in her dark hair and on her snowy bosom; her lovely face and slender lips were pale, and all the paler for the dusky glow of her eyes. She gazed at me with a strange, elusive smile; and yet there was, in her aspect and bearing, something familiar in the midst of strangeness, like the burden of a song heard long ago and recalled among other conditions and surroundings. It seemed to me that something in me recognized her and knew her, had known her always. She was the woman of whom I had dreamed, whom I had beheld in visions, whose voice and face had haunted me from boyhood up. Whether we had ever met before, as human beings meet, I knew not; perhaps I had been blindly seeking her all over the world, and she had been awaiting me in this splendid room, sitting by those dead embers until all the warmth had gone out of her blood, only to be restored by the heat with which my love might supply her.

"'I thought you had forgotten me,' she said, nodding as if in answer to my thought. 'The night was so late--our one night of the year! How my heart rejoiced when I heard your dear voice singing the song I know so well! Kiss me--my lips are cold!'

"Cold indeed they were--cold as the lips of death. But the warmth of my own seemed to revive them. They were now tinged with a faint color, and in her cheeks also appeared a delicate shade of pink. She drew fuller breath, as one who recovers from a long lethargy. Was it my life that was feeding her? I was ready to give her all. She drew me to the table and pointed to the viands and the wine.

"'Eat and drink,' she said. 'You have traveled far, and you need food.'

"'Will you eat and drink with me?' said I, pouring out the wine.

"'You are the only nourishment I want,' was her answer.' This wine is thin and cold. Give me wine as red as your blood and as warm, and I will drain a goblet to the dregs.'

"At these words, I know not why, a slight shiver passed through me. She seemed to gain vitality and strength at every instant, but the chill of the great room struck into me more and more.

"She broke into a fantastic flow of spirits, clapping her hands, and dancing about me like a child. Who was she? And was I myself, or was she mocking mo when she implied that we had belonged to each other of old? At length she stood still before me, crossing her hands over her breast. I saw upon the forefinger of her right hand the gleam of an antique ring.

"'Where did you get that ring?' I demanded.

"She shook her head and laughed. 'Have you been faithful?' she asked. 'It is my ring; it is the ring that unites us; it is the ring you gave me when you loved me first. It is the ring of the Kern--the fairy ring, and I am your Ethelind--Ethelind Fionguala.'

"'So be it,' I said, casting aside all doubt and fear, and yielding myself wholly to the spell of her inscrutable eyes and wooing lips. 'You are mine, and I am yours, and let us be happy while the hours last.'

"'You are mine, and I am yours,' she repeated, nodding her head with an elfish smile. 'Come and sit beside me, and sing that sweet song again that you sang to me so long ago. Ah, now I shall live a hundred years.'

"We seated ourselves on the ottoman, and while she nestled luxuriously among the cushions, I took my banjo and sang to her. The song and the music resounded through the lofty room, and came back in throbbing echoes. And before me as I sang I saw the face and form of Ethelind Fionguala, in her jeweled bridal dress, gazing at me with burning eyes. She was pale no longer, but ruddy and warm, and life was like a flame within her. It was I who had become cold and bloodless, yet with the last life that was in me I would have sung to her of love that can never die. But at length my eyes grew dim, the room seemed to darken, the form of Ethelind alternately brightened and waxed indistinct, like the last flickerings of a fire; I swayed toward her, and felt myself lapsing into unconsciousness, with my head resting on her white shoulder."

Here Keningale paused a few moments in his story, flung a fresh log upon the fire, and then continued:

"I awoke, I know not how long afterward. I was in a vast, empty room in a ruined building. Rotten shreds of drapery depended from the walls, and heavy festoons of spiders' webs gray with dust covered the windows, which were destitute of glass or sash; they had been boarded up with rough planks which had themselves become rotten with age, and admitted through their holes and crevices pallid rays of light and chilly draughts of air. A bat, disturbed by these rays or by my own movement, detached himself from his hold on a remnant of moldy tapestry near me, and after circling dizzily around my head, wheeled the flickering noiselessness of his flight into a darker corner. As I arose unsteadily from the heap of miscellaneous rubbish on which I had been lying, something which had been resting across my knees fell to the floor with a rattle. I picked it up, and found it to be my banjo--as you see it now.

"Well, that is all I have to tell. My health was seriously impaired; all the blood seemed to have been drawn out of my veins; I was pale and haggard, and the chill--Ah, that chill," murmured Keningale, drawing nearer to the fire, and spreading out his hands to catch the warmth--" I shall never get over it; I shall carry it to my grave."

"WHEN HALF-GODS GO, THE GODS ARRIVE."

"What a beautiful girl!" said Mr. Ambrose Drayton to himself; "and how much she looks like--" He cut the comparison short, and turned his eyes seaward, pulling at his mustache meditatively the while.

"This American atmosphere, fresh and pure as it is in the nostrils, is heavy-laden with reminiscences," his thoughts ran on. "Reminiscences, but always with differences, the chief difference being, no doubt, in myself. And no wonder. Nineteen years; yes, it's positively nineteen years since I stood here and gazed out through yonder gap between the headlands. Nineteen years of foreign lands, foreign men and manners, the courts, the camps, the schools; adventure, business, and pleasure-- if I may lightly use so mysterious a word. Nineteen and twenty are thirty-nine; in my case say sixty at least. Why, a girl like that lovely young thing walking away there with her light step and her innocent heart would take me to be sixty to a dead certainty. A rather well-preserved man of sixty--that's how she'd describe me to the young fellow she's given her heart to. Well, sixty or forty, what difference? When a man has passed the age at which he falls in love, he is the peer of Methuselah from that time forth. But what a fiery season that of love is while it lasts! Ay, and it burns something out of the soul that never grows again. And well that it should do so: a susceptible heart is a troublesome burden to lug round the world. Curious that I should be even thinking of such things: association, I suppose. Here it was that we met and here we parted. But what a different place it was then! A lovely cape, half bleak moorland and half shaggy wood, a few rocky headlands and a great many coots and gulls, and one solitary old farmhouse standing just where that spick-and-span summer hotel, with its balconies and cupolas, stands now. So it was nineteen years ago, and so it may be again, perhaps, nine hundred years hence; but meanwhile, what a pretty array of modern aesthetic cottages, and plank walks, and bridges, and bathing-houses, and pleasure-boats! And what an admirable concourse of well-dressed and pleasurably inclined men and women! After all, my country-men are the finest-looking and most prosperous-appearing people on the globe. They have traveled a little faster than I have, and on a somewhat different track; but

I would rather be among them than anywhere else. Yes, I won't go back to London, nor yet to Paris, or Calcutta, or Cairo. I'll buy a cottage here at Squittig Point, and live and die here and in New York. I wonder whether Mary is alive and mother of a dozen children, or--not!"

"Auntie," said Miss Leithe to her relative, as they regained the veranda of their cottage after their morning stroll on the beach, "who was that gentleman who looked at us?"

"Hey?--who?" inquired the widow of the late Mr. Corwin, absently.

"The one in the thin gray suit and Panama hat; you must have seen him. A very distinguished-looking man and yet very simple and pleasant; like some of those nice middle-aged men that you see in 'Punch,' slenderly built, with handsome chin and eyes, and thick mustache and whiskers. Oh, auntie, why do you never notice things? I think a man between forty and fifty is ever so much nicer than when they're younger. They know how to be courteous, and they're not afraid of being natural. I mean this one looks as if he would. But he must be somebody remarkable in some way--don't you think so? There's something about him--something graceful and gentle and refined and manly--that makes most other men seem common beside him. Who do you suppose he can be?"

"Who?--what have you been saying, my dear?" inquired Aunt Corwin, rousing herself from the perusal of a letter. "Here's Sarah writes that Frank Redmond was to sail from Havre the 20th; so he won't be here for a week or ten days yet."

"Well, he might not have come at all," said the girl, coloring slightly. "I'm sure I didn't think he would, when he went away."

"You are both of you a year older and wiser," said the widow, meditatively; "and you have learned, I hope, not to irritate a man needlessly. I never irritated Corwin in all my life. They don't understand it."

"Here comes Mr. Haymaker," observed Miss Leithe. "I shall ask him."

"Don't ask him in," said Mrs. Corwin, retiring; "he chatters like an organ-grinder."

"Oh, good-morning, Miss Mary!" exclaimed Mr. Haymaker, as he mounted the steps of the veranda, with his hands extended and his customary effusion. "How charming you are looking after your bath and your walk and all! Did you ever see such a charming morning? I never was at a place I liked so much as Squittig Point;

the new Newport, I call it-- eh? the new Newport. So fashionable already, and only been going, as one might say, three or four years! Such charming people here! Oh, by- the-way, whom do you think I ran across just now? You wouldn't know him, though--been abroad since before you were born, I should think. Most charming man I ever met, and awfully wealthy. Ran across him in Europe--Paris, I think it was--stop! or was it Vienna? Well, never mind. Drayton, that's his name; ever hear of him? Ambrose Drayton. Made a great fortune in the tea-trade; or was it in the mines? I've forgotten. Well, no matter. Great traveler, too--Africa and the Corea, and all that sort of thing; and fought under Garibaldi, they say; and he had the charge of some diplomatic affair at Pekin once. The quietest, most gentlemanly fellow you ever saw. Oh, you must meet him. He's come back to stay, and will probably spend the summer here. I'll get him and introduce him. Oh, he'll be charmed--we all shall."

"What sort of a looking person is he?" Miss Leithe inquired.

"Oh, charming--just right! Trifle above medium height; rather lighter weight than I am, but graceful; grayish hair, heavy mustache, blue eyes; style of a retired English colonel, rather. You know what I mean --trifle reticent, but charming manners. Stop! there he goes now--see him? Just stopping to light a cigar--in a line with the light-house. Now he's thrown away the match, and walking on again. That's Ambrose Drayton. Introduce him on the sands this afternoon. How is your good aunt to-day? So sorry not to have seen her! Well, I must be off; awfully busy to-day. Good-by, my dear Miss Mary; see you this afternoon. Good-by. Oh, make my compliments to your good aunt, won't you? Thanks. So charmed! *Au revoir*."

"Has that fool gone?" demanded a voice from within.

"Yes, Auntie," the young lady answered.

"Then come in to your dinner," the voice rejoined, accompanied by the sound of a chair being drawn up to a table and sat down upon. Mary Leithe, after casting a glance after the retreating figure of Mr. Haymaker and another toward the light-house, passed slowly through the wire-net doors and disappeared.

Mr. Drayton had perforce engaged his accommodations at the hotel, all the cottages being either private property or rented, and was likewise constrained, therefore, to eat his dinner in public. But Mr. Drayton was not a hater of his species, nor a fearer of it; and though he had not acquired precisely our American habits and customs, he was disposed to be as little strange to them as possible. Accordingly, when the gong sounded, he entered the large dining-room with great intrepidity. The arrangement of tables was not continuous, but many small tables, capable of accommodating from two to six, were dotted about everywhere. Mr. Drayton established himself at the smallest of them, situated in a part of the room whence he had a view not only of the room itself, but of the blue sea and yellow rocks on the other side. This preliminary feat of generalship accomplished, he took a folded dollar bill from his pocket and silently held it up in the air, the result being the speedy capture of a waiter and the introduction of dinner.

But at this juncture Mr. Haymaker came pitching into the room, as his nature was, and pinned himself to a standstill, as it were, with his eyeglass, in the central aisle of tables. Drayton at once gave himself up for lost, and therefore received Mr. Haymaker with kindness and serenity when, a minute or two later, he came plunging up, in his usual ecstasy of sputtering amiability, and seated himself in the chair at the other side of the table with an air as if everything were charming in the most charming of all possible worlds, and he himself the most charming person in it.

"My dear Drayton, though," exclaimed Mr. Haymaker, in the interval between the soup and the bluefish, "there is some one here you must know--most charming girl you ever knew in your life, and has set her heart on knowing you. We were talking about you this morning--Miss Mary Leithe. Lovely name, too; pity ever to change it--he! he! he! Why, you must have seen her about here; has an old aunt, widow of Jim Corwin, who's dead and gone these five years. You recognize her, of course?"

"Not as you describe her," said Mr. Drayton, helping his friend to fish.

"Oh, the handsomest girl about here; tallish, wavy brown hair, soft brown eyes, the loveliest-shaped eyes in the world, my dear fellow; complexion like a Titian, figure slender yet, but promising. A way of giving you her hand that makes you wish she would take your heart," pursued Mr. Haymaker, impetuously filling his mouth with bluefish, during the disposal of which he lost the thread of his harangue. Drayton, however, seemed disposed to recover it for him.

"Is this young lady from New England?" he inquired.

"New-Yorker by birth," responded the ever-vivacious Haymaker; "father a Southern man; mother a Bostonian. Father died eight or nine years after marriage;

mother survived him six years; girl left in care of old Mrs. Corwin--good old creature, but vague--very vague. Don't fancy the marriage was a very fortunate one; a
little friction, more or less. Leithe was rather a wild, unreliable sort of man; Mrs.
Leithe a woman not easily influenced--immensely charming, though, and all that,
but a trifle narrow and set. Well, you know, it was this way: Leithe was an im-
mensely wealthy man when she married him; lost his money, struggled along, good
deal of friction; Mrs. Leithe probably felt she had made a mistake, and that sort of
thing. But Miss Mary here, very different style, looks like her mother, but softer;
more in her, too. Very little money, poor girl, but charming. Oh! you must know
her."

"What did you say her mother's maiden name was?"

"Maiden name? Let me see. Why--oh, no--oh, yes--Cleveland, Mary Cleveland."

"Mary Cleveland, of Boston; married Hamilton Leithe, about nineteen years
ago. I used to know the lady. And this is her daughter! And Mary Cleveland is
dead!--Help yourself, Haymaker. I never take more than one course at this hour of
the day."

"But you must let me introduce you, you know," mumbled Haymaker, through
his succotash.

"I hardly know," said Drayton, rubbing his mustache. "Pardon me if I leave
you," he added, looking at his watch. "It is later than I thought."

Nothing more was seen of Drayton for the rest of that day. But the next morning, as Mary Leithe sat on the Bowlder Rock, with a book on her lap, and her eyes
on the bathers, and her thoughts elsewhere, she heard a light, leisurely tread behind her, and a gentlemanly, effective figure made its appearance, carrying a mal-
acca walking-stick, and a small telescope in a leather case slung over the shoulder.

"Good-morning, Miss Leithe," said this personage, in a quiet and pleasant voice.
"I knew your mother before you were born, and I can not feel like a stranger toward
her daughter. My name is Ambrose Drayton. You look something like your mother,
I think."

"I think I remember mamma's having spoken of you," said Mary Leithe, looking up a little shyly, but with a smile that was the most winning of her many winning manifestations. Her upper lip, short, but somewhat fuller than the lower one,

was always alive with delicate movements; the corners of her mouth were blunt, the teeth small; and the smile was such as Psyche's might have been when Cupid waked her with a kiss.

"It was here I first met your mother," continued Drayton, taking his place beside her. "We often sat together on this very rock. I was a young fellow then, scarcely older than you, and very full of romance and enthusiasm. Your mother--". He paused a moment, looking at his companion with a grave smile in his eyes. "If I had been as dear to her as she was to me," he went on, "you would have been our daughter."

Mary looked out upon the bathers, and upon the azure bay, and into her own virgin heart. "Are you married, too?" she asked at length.

"I was cut out for an old bachelor, and I have been true to my destiny," was his reply. "Besides, I've lived abroad till a month or two ago, and good Americans don't marry foreign wives."

"I should like to go abroad," said Mary Leithe.

"It is the privilege of Americans," said Drayton. "Other people are born abroad, and never know the delight of real travel. But, after all, America is best. The life of the world culminates here. We are the prow of the vessel; there may be more comfort amidships, but we are the first to touch the unknown seas. And the foremost men of all nations are foremost only in so far as they are at heart American; that is to say, America is, at present, even more an idea and a principle than it is a country. The nation has perhaps not yet risen to the height of its opportunities. So you have never crossed the Atlantic?"

"No; my father never wanted to go; and after he died, mamma could not."

"Well, our American Emerson says, you know, that, as the good of travel respects only the mind, we need not depend for it on railways and steamboats."

"It seems to me, if we never moved ourselves, our minds would never really move either."

"Where would you most care to go?"

"To Rome, and Jerusalem, and Egypt, and London."

"Why?"

"They seem like parts of my mind that I shall never know unless I visit them."

"Is there no part of the world that answers to your heart?"

"Oh, the beautiful parts everywhere, I suppose."

"I can well believe it," said Drayton, but with so much simplicity and straight-forwardness that Mary Leithe's cheeks scarcely changed color. "And there is beauty enough here," he added, after a pause.

"Yes; I have always liked this place," said she, "though the cottages seem a pity."

"You knew the old farm-house, then?"

"Oh, yes; I used to play in the farm-yard when I was a little girl. After my father died, Mamma used to come here every year. And my aunt has a cottage here now. You haven't met my aunt, Mr. Drayton?"

"I wished to know you first. But now I want to know her, and to become one of the family. There is no one left, I find, who belongs to me. What would you think of me for a bachelor uncle?"

"I would like it very much," said Mary, with a smile.

"Then let us begin," returned Drayton.

Several days passed away very pleasantly. Never was there a bachelor uncle so charming, as Haymaker would have said, as Drayton. The kind of life in the midst of which he found himself was altogether novel and delightful to him. In some aspects it was like enjoying for the first time a part of his existence which he should have enjoyed in youth, but had missed; and in many ways he doubtless enjoyed it more now than he would have done then, for he brought it to a maturity of experience which had taught him the inestimable value of simple things; a quiet nobility of character and clearness of knowledge that enabled him to perceive and follow the right course in small things as in great; a serene yet cordial temperament that rendered him the cheerfulest and most trustworthy of companions; a generous and masculine disposition, as able to direct as to comply; and years which could sympathize impartially with youth and age, and supply something which each lacked. He, meanwhile, sometimes seemed to himself to be walking in a dream. The region in which he was living, changed, yet so familiar, the thought of being once more, after so many years of homeless wandering, in his own land and among his own country-men, and the companionship of Mary Leithe, like, yet so unlike, the Mary Cleveland he had known and loved, possessing in reality all the tenderness and lovely virginal sweetness that he had imagined in the other, with a warmth of heart that rejuvenated his own, and a depth and freshness of mind answering to the wisdom that he had drawn from experience, and rendering her, though in her different and feminine sphere, his equal--all these things made Drayton feel as if he would either awake and find them the phantasmagoria of a beautiful dream, or as if the past time were the dream, and this the reality. Certainly, in this ardent, penetrating light of the present, the past looked vaporous and dim, like a range of mountains scaled long ago and vanishing on the horizon.

And was this all? Doubtless it was, at first. It was natural that Drayton should regard with peculiar tenderness the daughter of the woman he had loved. She was an orphan, and poor; he was alone in the world, with no one dependent upon him, and with wealth which could find no better use than to afford this girl the opportunities and the enjoyments which she else must lack. His anticipations in returning to America had been somewhat cold and vague. It was his native land; but abstract patriotism is, after all, rather chilly diet for a human being to feed his heart upon. The unexpected apparition of Mary Leithe had provided just that vividness and particularity that were wanting. Insensibly Drayton bestowed upon her all the essence of the love of country which he had cherished untainted throughout his long exile. It was so much easier and simpler a thing to know and appreciate her than to do as much for the United States and their fifty million inhabitants, national, political, and social, that it is no wonder if Drayton, as a modest and sane gentleman, preferred to make the former the symbol of the latter--of all, at least, that was good and lovable therein. At the same time, so clear-headed a man could scarcely have failed to be aware that his affection for Mary Leithe was not actually dependent upon the fact of her being an emblem. Upon what, then, was it dependent? Upon her being the daughter of Mary Cleveland? It was true that he had loved Mary Cleveland; but she had deliberately jilted him to marry a wealthier man, and was therefore connected with and responsible for the most painful as well as the most pleasurable episode of his early life. Mary Leithe bore some personal resemblance to her mother; but had she been as like her in character and disposition as she was in figure and feature, would Drayton, knowing what he knew, have felt drawn toward her? A man does not remain for twenty years under the influence of an unreasonable and mistaken passion. Drayton certainly had not, although his disappointment had kept him a bachelor all his life, and altered the whole course of his existence. But when we have once embarked upon a certain career, we continue in it long after the motive which started us has been forgotten. No; Drayton's regard for Mary Leithe must stand on its own basis, independent of all other considerations.

What, in the next place, was the nature of this regard? Was it merely avuncular, or something different? Drayton assured himself that it was the former. He was a man of the world, and had done with passions. The idea of his falling in love made him smile in a deprecatory manner. That the object of such love should be a girl eighteen years his junior rendered the suggestion yet more irrational. She was lustrous with lovable qualities, which he genially recognized and appreciated; nay, he might love her, but the love would be a quasi-paternal one, not the love that demands absolute possession and brooks no rivalry. His attitude was contemplative and beneficent, not selfish and exclusive. His greatest pleasure would be to see her married to some one worthy of her. Meantime he might devote himself to her freely and without fear.

And yet, once again, was he not the dupe of himself and of a convention? Was his the mood in which an uncle studies his niece, or even a father his daughter? How often during the day was she absent from his thoughts, or from his dreams at night? What else gave him so much happiness as to please her, and what would he not do to give her pleasure? Why was he dissatisfied and aimless when not in her presence? Why so full-orbed and complete when she was near? He was eighteen years the elder, but there was in her a fullness of nature, a balanced development, which went far toward annulling the discrepancy. Moreover, though she was young, he was not old, and surely he had the knowledge, the resources, and the will to make her life happy. There would be, he fancied, a certain poetical justice in such an issue. It would illustrate the slow, seemingly severe, but really tender wisdom of Providence. Out of the very ashes of his dead hopes would arise this gracious flower of promise. She would afford him scope for the employment of all those riches, moral and material, which life had brought him; she would be his reward for having lived honorably and purely for purity's and honor's sake. But why multiply reasons? There was justification enough; and true love knows nothing of justification. He loved her, then; and now, did she love him? This was the real problem--the mystery of a maiden's heart, which all Solomon's wisdom and Bacon's logic fail to elucidate. Drayton did what he could. Once he came to her with the news that he must be absent from an excursion which they had planned, and he saw genuine disappointment darken her sweet face, and her slender figure seem to droop. This was well as far as it went, but beyond that it proved nothing. Another time he gave her a curious little shell which he had picked up while they were rambling together along the beach, and some time afterward he accidently noticed that she was wearing it by a ribbon round her neck. This seemed better. Again, on a night when there was a social gathering at the hotel, he entered the room and sat apart at one of the windows, and as long as he remained there he felt that her gaze was upon him, and twice or thrice when he raised his eyes they were met by hers, and she smiled; and afterward, when he was speaking near her, he noticed that she disregarded what her companion of the moment was saying to her, and listened only to him. Was not all this encouragement? Nevertheless, whenever, presuming upon this, he hazarded less ambiguous demonstrations, she seemed to shrink back and appear strange and troubled. This behavior perplexed him; he doubted the evidence that had given him hope; feared that he was a fool; that she divined his love, and pitied him, and would have him, if at all, only out of pity. Thereupon he took himself sternly to task, and resolved to give her up.

It was a transparent July afternoon, with white and gray clouds drifting across a clear blue sky, and a southwesterly breeze roughening the dark waves and showing their white shoulders. Mary Leithe and Drayton came slowly along the rocks, he assisting her to climb or descend the more rugged places, and occasionally pausing with her to watch the white canvas of a yacht shiver in the breeze as she went about, or to question whether yonder flash amid the waves, where the gulls were hovering and dipping, were a bluefish breaking water. At length they reached a little nook in the seaward face, which, by often resorting to it, they had in a manner made their own. It was a small shelf in the rock, spacious enough for two to sit in at ease, with a back to lean against, and at one side a bit of level ledge which served as a stand or table. Before them was the sea, which, at high-water mark, rose to within three yards of their feet; while from the shoreward side they were concealed by the ascending wall of sandstone. Drayton had brought a cushion with him, which he arranged in Mary's seat; and when they had established themselves, he took a volume of Emerson's poems from his pocket and laid it on the rock beside him.

"Are you comfortable?" he asked.

"Yes; I wish it would be always like this--the weather, and the sun, and the time--so that we might stay here forever."

"Forever is the least useful word in human language," observed Drayton. "In the perspective of time, a few hours, or days, or years, seem alike inconsiderable."

"But it is not the same to our hearts, which live forever," she returned.

"The life of the heart is love," said Drayton.

"And that lasts forever," said Mary Leithe.

"True love lasts, but the object changes," was his reply.

"It seems to change sometimes," said she.

"But I think it is only our perception that is misled. We think we have found what we love; but afterward, perhaps, we find it was not in the person we supposed, but in some other. Then we love it in him; not because our heart has changed, but just because it has not."

"Has that been your experience?" Drayton asked, with a smile.

"Oh, I was speaking generally," she said, looking down.

"It may be the truth; but if so, it is a perilous thing to be loved."

"Perilous?"

"Why, yes. How can the lover be sure that he really is what his mistress takes him for? After all, a man has and is nothing in himself. His life, his love, his goodness, such as they are, flow into him from his Creator, in such measure as he is capable or desirous of receiving them. And he may receive more at one time than at another. How shall he know when he may lose the talismanic virtue that won her love--even supposing he ever possessed it?"

"I don't know how to argue," said Mary Leithe; "I can only feel when a thing is true or not--or when I think it is--and say what I feel."

"Well, I am wise enough to trust the truth of your feeling before any argument."

This assertion somewhat disconcerted Mary Leithe, who never liked to be confronted with her own shadow, so to speak. However, she seemed resolved on this occasion to give fuller utterance than usual to what was in her mind; so, after a pause, she continued, "It is not only how much we are capable of receiving from God, but the peculiar way in which each one of us shows what is in him, that makes the difference in people. It is not the talisman so much as the manner of using it that wins a girl's love. And she may think one manner good until she comes to know that another is better."

"And, later, that another is better still?"

"You trust my feeling less than you thought, you see," said Mary, blushing, and with a tremor of her lips.

"Perhaps I am afraid of trusting it too much," Drayton replied, fixing his eyes upon her. Then he went on, with a changed tone and manner: "This metaphysical discussion of ours reminds me of one of Emerson's poems, whose book, by-the-by, I brought with me. Have you ever read them?"

"Very few of them," said Mary; "I don't seem to belong to them."

"Not many people can eat them raw, I imagine," rejoined Drayton, laughing. "They must be masticated by the mind before they can nourish the heart, and some of them--However, the one I am thinking of is very beautiful, take it how you will. It is called, 'Give all to Love.' Do you know it!"

Mary shook her head.

"Then listen to it," said Drayton, and he read the poem to her. "What do you think of it?" he asked when he had ended.

"It is very short," said Mary, "and it is certainly beautiful; but I don't understand some parts of it, and I don't think I like some other parts."

"It is a true poem," returned Drayton; "it has a body and a soul; the body is beautiful, but the soul is more beautiful still; and where the body seems incomplete, the soul is most nearly perfect. Be loyal, it says, to the highest good you know; follow it through all difficulties and dangers; make it the core of your heart and the life of your soul; and yet, be free of it! For the hour may always be at hand when that good that you have lived for and lived in must be given up. And then-- what says the poet?

"'Though thou loved her as thyself,
As a self of purer clay,
Though her parting dims the day,
Stealing grace from all alive,
Heartily know,
When half-gods go,

The gods arrive.'"

There was something ominous in Drayton's tone, quiet and pleasant though it sounded to the ear, and Mary could not speak; she knew that he would speak again, and that his words would bring the issue finally before her.

He shut the book and put it in his pocket. For some time he remained silent, gazing eastward across the waves, which came from afar to break against the rock at their feet. A small white pyramidal object stood up against the horizon verge, and upon this Drayton's attention appeared to be concentrated.

"If you should ever decide to come," he said at length, "and want the services of a courier who knows the ground well, I shall be at your disposal."

"Come where?" she said, falteringly.

"Eastward. To Europe."

"You will go with me?"

"Hardly that. But I shall be there to receive you."

"You are going back?"

"In a month, or thereabouts."

"Oh, Mr. Drayton! Why?"

"Well, for several reasons. My coming here was an experiment. It might have succeeded, but it was made too late. I am too old for this young country. I love it, but I can be of no service to it. On the contrary, so far as I was anything, I should be in the way. It does not need me, and I have been an exile so long as to have lost my right to inflict myself upon it. Yet I am glad to have been here; the little time that I have been here has recompensed me for all the sorrows of my life, and I shall never forget an hour of it as long as I live."

"Are you quite sure that your country does not want you--need you?"

"I should not like my assurance to be made more sure."

"How can you know? Who has told you? Whom have you asked?"

"There are some questions which it is not wise to put; questions whose answers may seem ungracious to give, and are sad to hear."

"But the answer might not seem so. And how can it be given until you ask it?"

Drayton turned and looked at her. His face was losing its resolute composure, and there was a glow in his eyes and in his cheeks that called up an answering warmth in her own.

"Do you know where my country is?" he demanded, almost sternly.

"It is where you are loved and wanted most, is it not?" she said, breathlessly.

"Do not deceive yourself--nor me!" exclaimed Drayton, putting out his hand toward her, and half rising from the rock. "There is only one thing more to say."

A sea-gull flew close by them, and swept on, and in a moment was far away, and lost to sight. So in our lives does happiness come so near us as almost to brush our cheeks with its wings, and then pass on, and become as unattainable as the stars. As Mary Leithe was about to speak, a shadow cast from above fell across her face and figure. She seemed to feel a sort of chill from it, warm though the day was; and without moving her eyes from Drayton's face to see whence the shadow came, her expression underwent a subtle and sudden change, losing the fervor of a moment before, and becoming relaxed and dismayed. But after a moment Drayton looked up, and immediately rose to his feet, exclaiming, "Frank Redmond!"

On the rock just above them stood a young man, dark of complexion, with eager eyes, and a figure athletic and strong. As Drayton spoke his name, his countenance assumed an expression half-way between pleased surprise and jealous suspicion. Meanwhile Mary Leithe had covered her face with her hands.

"I'm sure I'd no idea you were here, Mr. Drayton," said the young man. "I was looking for Mary Leithe. Is that she?"

Mary uncovered her face, and rose to her feet languidly. She did not as yet look toward Redmond, but she said in a low voice, "How do you do, Frank? You--came so suddenly!"

"I didn't stop to think--that I might interrupt you," said he, drawing back a little and lifting his head.

Drayton had been observing the two intently, breathing constrainedly the while, and grasping a jutting point of rock with his hand as he stood. He now said, in a genial and matter-of-fact voice, "Well, Master Frank, I shall have an account to settle with you when you and my niece have got through your first greetings."

"Mary your niece!" cried Redmond, bewildered.

"My niece by courtesy; her mother was a dear friend of mine before Mary was born. And now it appears that she is the young lady, the dearest and loveliest ever heard of, about whom you used to rhapsodize to me in Dresden! Why didn't you tell me her name? By Jove, you young rogue, I've a good mind to refuse my consent to the match! What if I had married her off to some other young fellow, and you been left in the lurch! However, luckily for you, I haven't been able thus far to find any one who in my opinion--How do you do, Frank? You--came so suddenly!"

"I didn't stop to think--that I might interrupt you," said he, drawing back a little and lifting his head.

Drayton had been observing the two intently, breathing constrainedly the while, and grasping a jutting point of rock with his hand as he stood. He now said, in a genial and matter-of-fact voice, "Well, Master Frank, I shall have an account to settle with you when you and my niece have got through your first greetings."

"Mary your niece!" cried Redmond, bewildered.

"My niece by courtesy; her mother was a dear friend of mine before Mary was born. And now it appears that she is the young lady, the dearest and loveliest ever heard of, about whom you used to rhapsodize to me in Dresden! Why didn't you tell me her name? By Jove, you young rogue, I've a good mind to refuse my consent to the match! What if I had married her off to some other young fellow, and you been left in the lurch! However, luckily for you, I haven't been able thus far to find any one who in my opinion would suit her better. Come down here and shake hands, Frank, and then I'll leave you to make your excuses to Miss Leithe. And the next time you come back to her after a year's absence, don't frighten her heart into her mouth by springing out on her like a jack-in-the-box. Send a bunch of flowers or a signet-ring to tell her you are coming, or you may get a cooler reception than you'd like!"

"Ah! Ambrose Drayton," he sighed to himself as he clambered down the rocks alone, and sauntered along the shore, "there is no fool like an old fool. Where were your eyes that you couldn't have seen what was the matter? Her heart was fighting against itself all the time, poor child! And you, selfish brute, bringing to bear on her all your antiquated charms and fascinations--Heaven save the mark!--and bullying her into the belief that you could make her happy! Thank God, Ambrose Drayton, that your awakening did not come too late. A minute more would have made her and you miserable for life--and Redmond too, confound him! And yet they might have told me; one of them might have told me, surely. Even at my age it is hard to remember one's own insignificance. And I did love her! God knows how I loved her! I hope he loves her as much; but how can he help it! And she--she won't re-member long! An old fellow who made believe he was her uncle, and made rather a fool of himself; went back to Europe, and never been heard of since. Ah, me!"

"Where did you get acquainted with Mr. Drayton, Frank?"

"At Dresden. It was during the vacation at Freiberg last winter, and I had come over to Dresden to have a good time. We stayed at the same hotel. We played a game of billiards together, and he chatted with me about America, and asked me about my mining studies at Freiberg; and I thought him about the best fellow I'd ever met. But I didn't know then --I hadn't any conception what a splendid fellow he really was. If ever I hear anybody talking of their ideal of a gentleman, I shall ask them if they ever met Ambrose Drayton."

"What did he do?"

"Well, the story isn't much to my credit; if it hadn't been for him, you might never have heard of me again; and it will serve me right to confess the whole thing to you. It's about a--woman."

"What sort of a woman?"

"She called herself a countess; but there's no telling what she really was. I only know she got me into a fearful scrape, and if it hadn't been for Mr. Drayton--"

"Did you do anything wrong, Frank?"

"No; upon my honor as a gentleman! If I had, Mary, I wouldn't be here now."

Mary looked at him with a sad face. "Of course I believe you, Frank," she said. "But I think I would rather not hear any more about it."

"Well, I'll only tell you what Mr. Drayton did. I told him all about it --how it began, and how it went on, and all; and how I was engaged to a girl in America--I didn't tell him your name; and I wasn't sure, then, whether you'd ever marry me, after all; because, you know, you had been awfully angry with me before I went away, because I wanted to study in Europe instead of staying at home. But, you see, I've got my diploma, and that'll give me a better start than I ever should have had if I'd only studied here. However--what was I saying? Oh! so he said he would find out about the countess, and talk to her himself. And how he managed I don't know; and he gave me a tremendous hauling over the coals for having been such an idiot; but it seems that instead of being a poor injured, deceived creature, with a broken heart, and all that sort of thing, she was a regular adventuress--an old hand at it, and had got lots of money out of other fellows for fear she would make a row. But Mr. Drayton had an interview with her. I was there, and I never shall forget it if I live to a hundred. You never saw anybody so quiet, so courteous, so resolute, and so immitigably stern as he was. And yet he seemed to be stern only against the wrong she was trying to do, and to be feeling kindness and compassion for her all the time. She tried everything she knew, but it wasn't a bit of use, and at last she broke down and cried, and carried on like a child. Then Mr. Drayton took her out of the room, and I don't know what happened, but I've always suspected that he sent her off with money enough in her pocket to become an honest woman with if she chose to; but he never would admit it to me. He came back to me after a while, and told me to have nothing more to do with any woman, good or bad except the woman I meant to marry, and I promised him I wouldn't, and I kept my promise. But we have him to thank for our happiness, Mary."

Tears came silently into Mary's eyes; she said nothing, but sat with her hands clasped around one knee, gazing seaward.

"You don't seem very happy, though," pursued Redmond, after a pause; "and you acted so oddly when I first found you and Mr. Drayton together--I almost thought--well, I didn't know what to think. You do love me, don't you?"

For a few moments Mary Leithe sat quite motionless, save for a slight tremor of the nerves that pervaded her whole body; and then, all at once, she melted into sobs. Redmond could not imagine what was the matter with her; but he put his arms round her, and after a little hesitation or resistance, the girl hid her face upon his shoulder, and wept for the secret that she would never tell.

But Mary Leithe's nature was not a stubborn one, and easily adapted itself to the influences with which she was most closely in contact. When she and Redmond presented themselves at Aunt Corwin's cottage that evening her tears were dried, and only a tender dimness of the eyes and a droop of her sweet mouth betrayed that she had shed any.

"Mr. Drayton wanted to be remembered to you, Mary," observed Aunt Corwin, shortly before going to bed. She had been floating colored sea- weeds on paper all the time since supper, and had scarcely spoken a dozen words.

"Has he gone?" Mary asked.

"Who? Oh, yes; he had a telegram, I believe. His trunks were to follow him.

He said he would write. I liked that man. He was not like Mr. Haymaker; he was a gentleman. He took an interest in my collections, and gave me several nice specimens. Your mother was a fool not to have married him. I wish you could have married him yourself. But it was not to be expected that he would care for a child like you, even if your head were not turned by that Frank Redmond. How soon shall you let him marry you?"

"Whenever he likes," answered Mary Leithe, turning away.

As a matter of fact, they were married the following winter. A week before the ceremony a letter arrived for Mary from New York, addressed in a legal hand. It contained an intimation that, in accordance with the instructions of their client, Mr. Ambrose Drayton, the undersigned had placed to her account the sum of fifty thousand dollars as a preliminary bequest, it being the intention of Mr. Drayton to make her his heir. There was an inclosure from Drayton himself, which Mary, after a moment's hesitation, placed in her lover's hand, and bade him break the seal.

It contained only a few lines, wishing happiness to the bride and bridegroom, and hoping they all might meet in Europe, should the wedding trip extend so far. "And as for you, my dear niece," continued the writer, "whenever you think of me remember that little poem of Emerson's that we read on the rocks the last time I saw you. The longer I live the more of truth do I find in it, especially in the last verse:

"'Heartily know,
When half-gods go,
The gods arrive!'"

"What does that mean?" demanded Redmond, looking up from the letter.

"We can not know except by experience," answered Mary Leithe.

"SET NOT THY FOOT ON GRAVES."

***New York**, April 29th*.--Last night I came upon this passage in my old author: "Friend, take it sadly home to thee--Age and Youthe are strangers still. Youthe, being ignorant of the wisdome of Age, which is Experience, but wise with its own wisdome, which is of the unshackeled Soule, or Intuition, is great in Enterprise, but slack in Achievement. Holding itself equal to all attempts and conditions, and to be heir, not of its own spanne of yeares and compasse of Faculties only, but of all time and all Human Nature--such, I saye, being its illusion (if, indeede, it be illusion, and not in some sorte a Truth), it still underrateth the value of Opportunitie, and, in the vain beleefe that the City of its Expectation is paved with Golde and walled with Precious Stones, letteth slip betwixt its fingers those diamondes and treasures which ironical Fate offereth it.... But see nowe what the case is when this youthe becometh in yeares. For nowe he can nowise understand what defecte of Judgmente (or effecte of insanitie rather) did leade him so to despise and, as it were, reject those Giftes and golden chaunces which come but once to mortal men. Experience (that saturnine Pedagogue) hath taught him what manner of man he is, and that, farre from enjoying that Deceptive Seeminge or mirage of Freedome which would persuade him that he may run hither and thither as the whim prompteth over the face of the Earthe--yea, take the wings of the morninge and winnowe his aerie way to the Pleiadies-- he must e'en plod heavilie and with paine along that single and narrowe Path whereto the limitations of his personal nature and profession confine him--happy if he arrive with muche diligence and faire credit at the ende thereof, and falle not ignobly by the way. Neverthelesse-- for so great is the infatuation of man, who, although he acquireth all other knowledge, yet arriveth not at the knowledge of Himself--if to the Sage of Experience he proffered once again the gauds and prizes of youthe, which he hath ever since regretted and longed for--what doeth he in his wisdome? Verilie, so longe as the matter remaineth *in nubibis*, as the Latins say, or in the Region of the Imagination, as oure speeche hath it, he will beleeve, yea, take his oathe, that he still is master of all those capacities and energies whiche, in his youthe, would have prompted and enabled him to profit by this desired occurrence. Yet shall it appeare (if the thinge be brought still further to the teste, and, from an Imagination or Dreame, become an actual Realitie), that he will shrinke from and decline that which he did erste so ardently sigh for and covet. And the reason of this is as follows, to-wit: That Habit or Custome hath brought him more to love and affect those very ways and conditions of life, yea, those inconveniences and deficiencies which he useth to deplore and abhorre, than that Crown of Golde or Jewel of Happiness whose withholding he hath all his life lamented. Hence we may learne, that what is past, is dead, and that though thoughts be free, nature is ever captive, and loveth her chaine."

This is too lugubrious and cynical not to have some truth in it; but I am unwilling to believe that more than half of it is true. The author himself was evidently an old man, and therefore a prejudiced judge; and he did not make allowances for the range and variety of temperament. Age is not a matter of years, and scarcely of experience. The only really old persons are the selfish ones. The man whose thoughts, actions, and affections center upon himself, soon acquires a fixity and crustiness which (if to be old is to be "strange to youth") is old as nothing else is. But the man who makes the welfare and happiness of others his happiness, is as young at threescore as he was at twenty, and perhaps even younger, for he has had no time to grow old.

April 30th.--The Courtneys are in town! This is, I believe, her first visit to America since he married her. At all events, I have not seen or heard of her in all these seven years. I wonder ... I was going to write, I wonder whether she remembers me. Of course she remembers me, in a sort of way. I am tied up somewhere among her bundle of recollections, and occasionally, in an idle moment, her eye falls upon me, and moves her, perhaps, to smile or to sigh. For my own part, in thinking over our old days, I find I forget her less than I had supposed. Probably she has been more or less consciously in my mind throughout. In the same way, one has always latent within him the knowledge that he must die; but it does not follow that he is continually musing on the thought of death. As with death, so with this old love of mine. What a difference, if we had married! She was a very lovely girl--at least, I thought so then. Very likely I should not think her so now. My taste and knowledge have developed; a different order of things interests me. It may not be an altogether pleasant thing to confess; but, knowing myself as I now do, I have often thanked my stars that I am a bachelor.

Doubtless she is even more changed than I am. A woman changes more than a man in seven years, and a married woman especially must change a great deal from twenty-two to twenty-nine. Think of Ethel Leigh being in her thirtieth year! and the mother of four or five children, perhaps. Well, for the matter of that, think of the romantic and ambitious young Claude Campbell being an old bachelor of forty! I have married Art instead of Ethel, and she, instead of being Mrs. Campbell, is Mrs. Courtney.

It was a surprising thing--her marrying him so suddenly. But, appearances to the contrary notwithstanding, I have never quite made up my mind that Ethel was really fickle. She did it out of pique, or pride, or impulse, or whatever it is that sways women in such cases. She was angry, or indignant--how like fire and ice at once she was when she was angry!--and she was resolved to show me that she could do without me. She would not listen to my explanations; and I was always awkward and stiff about making explanations. Besides, it was not an easy matter to explain, especially to a girl like her. With a married woman or a widow it would have been a simple thing enough. But Ethel Leigh, the minister's daughter--innocent, ignorant, passionate--she would tolerate nothing short of a public disavowal and discontinuance of my relations with Mrs. Murray, and that, of course, I could not consent to, though heaven knows (and so must Ethel, by this time) that Mrs. Murray was nothing to me save as she was the wife of my friend, during whose enforced absence I was bound to look after her, to some extent. It was not my fault that poor Mrs. Murray was a fool. But such are the trumpery seeds from which tragedies grow. Not that ours was a tragedy, exactly: Ethel married her English admirer, and I became a somewhat distinguished artist, that is all. I wonder whether she has been happy! Likely enough; she was born to be wealthy; Englishmen make good husbands sometimes, and her London life must have been a brilliant one.... I have been looking at my old photograph of her--the one she gave me the morning after we were engaged. Tall, slender, dark, with level brows, and the bearing of a Diana. She certainly was handsome, and I shall not run the risk of spoiling this fine memory by calling on her. Even if she have not deteriorated, she can scarcely have improved. Nay, even were she the same now as then, I should not find her so, because of the change in myself. Why should I blink the truth? Experience, culture, and the sober second thought of middle age have carried me far beyond the point where I could any longer be in sympathy with this crude, thin-skinned, impulsive girl. And then--four or five children! Decidedly, I will give her a wide berth. And Courtney himself, with his big beard, small brain, and obtrusive laugh! I shall step across to California for a few months.

May 1st.--Called this morning on Ethel Leigh--Mrs. Deighton Courtney, that is to say. She is not so much changed, but she has certainly improved. When I say she has not changed much, I refer to her physical appearance. Her features are scarcely altered; her figure is a little fuller and more compact; in her bearing there is a certain quiet composure and self-possession--the air of a woman who has seen the world, has received admiration, and is familiar with the graceful little arts of social intercourse. In short, she has acquired a high external polish; and that is precisely what she most needed. Evidently, too, there is an increased mental refinement corresponding to the outward manner. She has mellowed, sweetened--whether deepened or not I should hesitate to affirm. But I am quite sure that I find her more charming to talk with, more supple in intercourse, more fascinating, in a word, than formerly. We chatted discursively and rather volubly for more than an hour; yet we did not touch on anything very serious or profound. They are staying at the Brevoort House. Courtney himself, by- the-by, is still in Boston (they landed there), where business will detain him a few days. Ethel goes on a house-hunting expedition to- morrow, and I am going with her; for New York has altered out of her recollection during these seven years. They are to remain here three years, perhaps longer. Courtney is to establish and oversee an American branch of his English business.

They have only one child--a pretty little thing: Susie and I became great friends.

Mrs. Courtney opened the door of the private sitting-room in which I was awaiting her, and came in--beautifully! She has learned how to do that since I knew her. My own long residence in Paris has made me more critical than I used to be in such matters; but I do not remember having met any woman in society with manners more nearly perfect than Mrs. Courtney's. Ethel Leigh used to be, upon occasion, painfully abrupt and disconcerting; and her movements and attitudes, though there was abundant native grace in them, were often careless and unconventional. Of course, I do not forget that niceties of deportment, without sound qualities of mind and heart to back them, are of trifling value; but the two kinds of attraction are by no means incompatible with each other. Mrs. Courtney smiles often. Ethel Leigh used to smile rarely, although, when the smile did come, it was irresistibly winning; there was in it exquisite significance and tenderness. It is a beautiful smile still, but that charm of rarity (if it be a charm) is lacking. It is a conventional smile more than a spontaneous or a happy one; indeed, it led me to surmise that she had perhaps not been very happy since we last met, and had learned to use this smile as a sort of veil. Not that I suppose for a moment that Courtney has ill-treated her. I never could see anything in the man beyond a superficial comeliness, a talent for business, and an affable temper; but ho was not in any sense a bad fellow. Besides, he was over head and ears in love with her; and Ethel would be sure to have the upper hand of a nature like his. No, her unhappiness, if she be unhappy, would be due to no such cause, she and her husband are no doubt on good terms with each other. But--suppose she has discovered that he fell short of what she demanded in a husband; that she overmatched him; that, in order to make their life smooth, she must descend to him? I imagine it may be something of that kind. Poor Mrs. Courtney!

She addressed me as "Mr. Campbell," and I dare say she was right. Women best know how to meet these situations. To have called me "Claude" would have placed us in a false position, by ignoring the changes that have taken place. It is wise to respect these barriers; they are conventional, but, rightly considered, they are more of an assistance than of an obstacle to freedom of intercourse. I asked her how she liked England. She smiled and said, "It was my business to like England; still, I am glad to see America once more."

"You will entertain a great deal, I presume--that sort of thing?"

"We shall hope to make friends with people--and to meet old friends. It is such a pleasant surprise to find you here. I heard you were settled in Paris."

"So I was, for several years; the Parisians said nice things about my pictures. But one may weary even of Paris. I returned here two years ago, and am now as much of a fixture in New York as if I'd never left it."

"But not a permanent fixture. Shall we never see you in London?"

"My present probabilities lie rather in the direction of California. I want to make some studies of the scenery and the atmosphere. Besides, I am getting too old to think of another European residence."

"No one gets old after thirty--especially no bachelor!" she answered, with a smile. "But if you were ever to feel old, the society of London would rejuvenate you."

"It has certainly done you no harm. But you have the happiness to be married."

She looked at me pleasantly and said, "Yes, I make a good Englishwoman." That sounded like an evasion, but the expression of her face was not evasive. In the old days she would probably have flushed up and said something cutting.

"You must see my little girl," she said, after a while.

The child was called, and presently came in. She resembles her mother, and has a vivacity scarcely characteristic of English children. I am not constitutionally a worshiper of children, but I liked Susie. She put her arms round her mother's arm, and gazed at me with wide-eyed scrutiny."

"This is Mr. Campbell," said mamma.

"My name is Susan Courtney," said the little thing. "We are going to stay in New York three years. Hot here--this is only an hotel--we are going to have a house. How do you do? This is my dolly."

I saluted dolly, and thereby inspired its parent with confidence: she put her hand in mine, and gave me her smooth little cheek to kiss. "You are not like papa," she then observed.

I smiled conciliatingly, being uncertain whether it were prudent to follow this lead; but Mrs. Courtney asked, "In what way different, dear?"

"Papa has a beard," replied Susie.

The incident rather struck me; it seemed to indicate that Mrs. Courtney was under no apprehension that the child would say anything embarrassing about the father. Having learned so much, I ventured farther.

"Do you love papa or mamma best?" I inquired.

"I am with mamma most," she answered, after meditation, "but when papa comes, I like him."

This was non-committal. She continued, "Papa is coming here day after to-morrow. To-morrow, mamma and I are going to find a house."

"Your husband leaves all that to you?" I said, turning to Mrs. Courtney.

"Mr. Courtney never knows or cares what sort of a place he lives in. It took me some little time to get used to that. I wanted everything to be just in a certain way. They used to laugh at me, and say I was more English than he."

"Now that you are both here, you must both be American."

"He doesn't enjoy America much. Of course, it is very different from London. An Englishman can not be expected to care for American ways and American quickness, and--"

"American people?" I put in, laughingly.

"Don't undress dolly here," she said to Susie. "It isn't time yet to put her to bed, and she might catch cold."

Was this another evasion? The serene face betrayed nothing, but she had left unanswered the question that aimed at discovering how she and her husband stood toward each other. After all, however, no answer could have told me more than her no answer did--supposing it to have been intentional. I soon afterward took my leave, after having arranged to call to-morrow and accompany her and Susie on their house-hunting expedition. Upon the whole, I don't think I am sorry to have renewed my acquaintance with her. She is more delightful--as an acquaintance--than when I knew her formerly. Should I have fallen in love with her had I met her for the first time as she is now? Yes, and no! In the old days there was something about her that commanded me--that fascinated my youthful imagination. Perhaps it was only the freshness, the ignorance, the timidity of young maidenhood--that mystery of possibilities of a nature that has not yet met the world and received its impress for good or evil. It is this which captivates in youth; and this, of course, Mrs. Courtney has lost. But every quality that might captivate mature manhood is hers, and, were I likely to think of marriage now, and were she marriageable, she is the type of woman I would choose. Yet I do not quite relish the perception that my present feminine ideal (whether it be lower or higher) is not the former one. But,--frankly, would I marry her if I could? I hardly know: I have got out of the habit of regarding marriage as among my possibilities; many avenues of happiness that once were open to me are now closed against me. Put it, that I have lost a faculty--that I am now able to enjoy only in imagination a phase of existence that, formerly, I could have enjoyed in fact. This bit of self-analysis may be erroneous; but I would not like to run the risk of proving it so! Am I not well enough off as I am? My health is fair, my mind active, my reputation secure, my finances prosperous. The things that I can dream must surely be better than anything that could happen. I can picture, for example, a state of matrimonial felicity which no marriage of mine could realize. Besides, I can, whenever I choose, see Mrs. Courtney herself, talk with her, and enjoy her as a reasonable and congenial friend, apart from the danger and disappointment that might result from a closer connection. I think I have chosen the wiser part, or, rather, the wiser part has been thrust upon me. That I shall never be wildly happy is, at least, security that I shall never be profoundly miserable. I shall simply be comfortable. Is this sour grapes? Am I, if not counting, then discounting my eggs before they are hatched? To such questions a practical--a materialized-- answer would be the only conclusive one. Were Mrs. Courtney ready to drop into my mouth, I should either open my mouth, or else I should shut it, and either act would be conclusive. But, so far from being ready to drop into my mouth, she is immovably and (to all appearances) contentedly fixed where she is. I suppose I am insinuating that appearances are deceptive; that she may be unhappy with her husband, and desire to leave him. Well, there is no technical evidence in support of such an hypothesis; but, again, in a matter of this kind, it is not so much the technical as the indirect evidence that tells--the cadences of the voice, the breathing, the silences, the atmosphere. There is no denying that I did somehow acquire a vague impression that Courtney is not so large a figure in his wife's eyes as he might be. I may have been biased by my previous conception of his character, or I may have misinterpreted the impalpable, indescribable signs that I remarked in her. But, once more, how do I know that her not caring for him would postulate her caring for me? Why should she care for either of us? Our old romance is to her as the memory of something read in a book, and it is powerless to make her heart beat one throb the faster. Were Courtney to die to-morrow, would his widow expect me to marry her? Not she! She would settle down here quietly, educate her daughter, and think better of her departed husband with every year that passed, and less of repeating the experiment that made her his! I may be prone to romantic and elaborate specu- lations, but I am not exactly a fool. I do not delude myself with the idea that Mrs. Courtney is, at this moment, following my example by recording her impressions of me at her own writing-desk, and asking herself whether--if such and such a thing were to happen--such another would be apt to follow. No; she has put Susie to bed, and is by this time asleep herself, after having read through the "Post," or "Bazar," or the last new novel, as her predilection may be. It is after midnight; since she has not followed my example, I will follow hers; it is much the more sensible of the two.

May 2d.--What a woman she is! and, in a different sense, what a man I am! How little does a man know or suspect himself until he is brought to the proof! How serenely and securely I philosophized and laid down the law yesterday! and to-day, how strange to contrast the event with my prognostication of it! And yet, again, how little has happened that might not be told in such a way as to appear nothing! It was the latent meaning, the spirit, the touch of look and tone. Her husband may have reached New York by this time; they may be together at this moment; he will find no perceptible change in her--perceptible to him! He will be told that I have been her escort during the day, and that I was polite and serviceable, and that a house has been selected. What more is there to tell? Nothing--that he could hear or understand! and yet--everything! He will say, "Yes, I recollect Campbell; nice fellow; have him to dine with us one of these days." But I shall never sit at their table; I shall never see her again; I can not! I shall start for California next week. Meanwhile I will write down the history of one day, for it is well to have these things set visibly before one --to grasp the nettle, as it were. Nothing is so formidable as it appears when we shrink from defining it to ourselves.

I drove to the hotel in my brougham at eleven o'clock, as we had previously arranged. She was ready and waiting for me, and little Susie was with her. Ethel was charmingly dressed, and there was a soft look in her eyes as she turned them on me--a look that seemed to say, "I remember the past; it is pleasant to see you, so pleasant as to be sad!" Susie came to me as if I were an old friend, and I lifted the child from the floor and kissed her twice.

"Why did you give me two kisses?" she demanded, as I put her down. "Papa always gives me only one kiss."

"Papa has mamma as well as you to kiss; but I have no one; I am an old bachelor."

"When you have known mamma longer, will you kiss her too?"

"Old bachelors kiss nobody but little girls," I replied, laughing.

"We went down to the brougham, and after we were seated and on our way," Ethel said, "Already I feel so much at home in New York, it almost startles me. I fancied I should have forgotten old associations--should have grown out of sympathy with them; but I seem only to have learned to appreciate them more. Our memory for some things is better than we would believe."

"There are two memories in us," I remarked; "the memory of the heart and the memory of the head. The former never is lost, though the other may be. But I had not supposed that you cared very deeply for the American period of your life."

"England is very agreeable," she said, rather hastily. She turned her head and looked out of the window; but after a pause she added, as if to herself, "but I am an American!"

"There is, no doubt, a deep-rooted and substantial repose in English life such as is scarcely to be found elsewhere," I said; "but, for all that, I have often thought that the best part of domestic happiness could exist nowhere but here. Here a man may marry the woman he loves, and their affection for each other will be made stronger by the hardships they may have to pass through. After all, when we come to the end of our lives, it is not the business we have done, nor the social distinction we have enjoyed--it is the love we have given and received that we are glad of."

"Mamma," inquired Susie, "does Mr. Campbell love you?"

We both of us looked at the child and laughed a little. "Mr. Campbell is an old friend," said Ethel. After a few moments she blushed. She held in her hand some house-agents' orders to view houses, and these she now began to examine. "Is this Madison Avenue place likely to be a good one?" she asked me.

"It is conveniently situated and comfortable; but I should think it might be too large for a family of three. Perhaps, though, you don't like a close fit?"

"I don't like empty rooms, though I prefer such rooms as there are to be large. But it doesn't make much difference. Mr. Courtney moves about a good deal, and he is as happy in a hotel as anywhere. These American hotels are luxurious and splendid, but they are not home-like to me."

"I remember you used to dislike being among a crowd of people you didn't know."

"Yes, and I haven't yet learned to be sociable in that way. A friend is more company for me than a score of acquaintances. Dear me! I'm afraid New York will spoil me--for England!"

"Perhaps Mr. Courtney may be cured of England by New York."

She smiled and said, "Perhaps! He accommodates himself to things more easily than I do, but I think one needs to be born in America to know how to love it."

Under the veil of discussing America and things in general, we were talking of ourselves, awakening reminiscences of the past, and discovering, with a pleasure we did not venture to acknowledge, that-- allowing for the events and the years that had come between--we were as much in accord as when we were young lovers. Yes, as much, and perhaps even more. For surely, if one grows in the right way, the sphere of knowledge and sympathy must enlarge, and thereby the various points of contact between two minds and hearts must be multiplied. Ethel and I, during these seven years, had traveled our round of daily life on different sides of the earth; but the miles of sea and land which had physically separated us had been powerless to estrange our spirits. Nothing is more strange, in this mysterious complexity of impressions and events that we call human existence, than the fact that two beings, entirely cut off from all natural means of association and communion, may yet, unknown to each other, be breathing the same spiritual air and learning the same moral and intellectual lessons. Like two seeds of the same species, planted, the one in American soil, the other in English, Ethel and I had selected, by some instinct of the soul, the same elements from our different surroundings; so that now, when we met once more, we found a close and harmonious resemblance between the leaves and blossoms of our experience. What can be more touching and delightful than such a discovery? Or what more sad than to know that it came too late for us to profit by it?

Oh, Ethel, how easy it is to take the little step that separates light from darkness, happiness from misery! Remembering that we live but once, and that the worthy enjoyments of life are so limited in number and so hard to get, it seems unjust and monstrous that one little hour of jealousy or misunderstanding should wreck the fair prospects of months and years. Why is mischief so much readier to our hand than good?

We got out at a house near the Park. I assisted Ethel to alight, and, as her hand rested on mine, the thought crossed my mind--How sweet if this were our own home that we are about to enter!--and I glanced at her face to see whether a like thought had visited her. She maintained a subdued demeanor, with an expression about the mouth and eyes of a peculiar timid gentleness, and, as it were, a sort of mental leaning upon me for support and protection. She felt, it may be, a little fear of herself, at finding herself--in more senses than one--so near to me; and, woman-like, she depended upon me to protect her against the very peril of which I was the occasion. No higher or more delicate compliment can be paid by a woman to a man; and I resolved that I would do what in me lay to deserve it. But such resolutions are the hardest in the world to keep, because the circumstance or the impulse of the moment is continually in wait to betray you. Ethel was more fascinating and lovely in this mood than in any other I had hitherto seen her in; and the misgiving, from which I could not free myself, that the man whom Fate had made her husband did not appreciate or properly cherish the gift bestowed upon him, made me warm toward her more than ever. I could scarcely have believed that such blood could flow in the sober veins of my middle age; but love knows nothing of time or age!

"I do not like this house," Susie declared, when we had been admitted by the care-taker. "It has no carpets, nor chairs, nor pictures; and the floor is dirty; and the walls are not pretty!"

"I suppose one can have these houses decorated and furnished at short notice?" Ethel asked me.

"It would not take long. There are several firms that make it their specialty."

"I have always wanted to live in a house where the colors and forms were to my taste. I don't know whether you remember that you used to think I had some taste in such matters. Mr. Courtney, of course, doesn't care much about art, and he didn't encourage me to carry out my ideas. A business man can not be an artist, you know."

"You yourself would have become an artist if--" I began; but I was approaching dangerous ground, and I stopped. "This dining-room might be done in Indian red," I remarked--"the woodwork, that is to say. The walls would be a warm salmon color, which contrasts well with the cold blue of the china, which it is the fashion to have about nowadays. As for the furniture, antique dark oak is as safe as anything, don't you think so?"

"I should like all that," said she, moving a little nearer me, and letting her eyes wander about the room with a pleased expression, until at length they met my own. "If you could only design our decoration for us, I'm sure it would be perfect; at least, I should be satisfied. Well, and how should we... how ought the drawing-room to be done?"

"There is a shade of yellow that is very agreeable for drawing-rooms, and it goes very well with the dull peacock-blue which is in vogue now. Then you could get one of those bloomy Morris friezes. There is some very graceful Chippendale to be picked up in various places. And no such good furniture is made nowadays. But I am advising you too much from the artist's point of view."

"Oh, I can get other sort of advice when I want it." She looked at me with a smile; our glances met more often now than at first. "But it seems to me," she went on, "that the way the house is built docs not suit the way we want to decorate it. Let us look at a smaller one. I should think ten rooms would be quite enough. And it would be nice to have a corner house, would it not?"

"If the question were only of our agreement, there would probably not be much difficulty," I said, in a tone which I tried to make merely courteous, but which may have revealed something more than courtesy beneath it.

In coming down-stairs she gathered her dress in her right hand and put her left in my arm; and then, in a flash, the picture came before me of the last time we had gone arm-in-arm together down-stairs. It was at her father's house, and she was speaking to me of that unlucky Mrs. Murray; we had our quarrel that evening in the drawing-room, and it was never made up. From then till now, what a gulf! and yet those years would have been but a bridge to pass over, save for the one barrier that was insurmountable between us.

"What has become of that Mrs. Murray whom you used to know?" she asked, as we reached the foot of the stairs. She relinquished my arm as she spoke, and faced me.

I felt the blood come to my face. "Mrs. Murray was in my thoughts at the same moment--and perhaps by the same train of associations." I answered, "I don't know where she is now; I lost sight of her years ago--soon after you were married, in fact. Why do you ask?"

"You had not forgotten her, then?"

"I had every reason to forget her, except the one reason for which I have remembered her--and you know what that is! Have you mistrusted me all this time?"

"Oh, no--no! I don't think I really mistrusted you at all; and long ago I admitted to myself that you had acted unselfishly and honorably. But I was angry at the time; you know, sometimes a girl will be angry, even when there is no good reason for it. I have long wished for an opportunity to tell you this, for my own sake, you know, as well as for yours."

"I hardly know whether I am most glad or sorry to hear this," I said, as we moved toward the door. "If you had only been able to say it, or to think it, before ... there would have been a great difference!"

"The worst of mistakes is, they are so seldom set right at the time, or in the way they ought to be. Come, Susie, we are going away now. Susie, do you most like to be American or English?"

"English," replied Susie, without hesitation.

Her mother turned to me and said in a low tone:

"I love her, whichever she is."

I understood what she meant. Susie was the symbol of that inevitable element in our lives which seems to evolve itself without reference to our desires or efforts; but which, nevertheless, when we have recognized that it is inevitable, we learn (if we are wise) to accept and even to love. Save for the estrangement between Ethel and myself, Susie would never have existed; yet there she was, a beautiful child, who had as good a right to be as either of us; and her mother loved her, and, as it were, bade me love her also. I took the little maiden by the hand and said, "You are right, Susie; the Americans are the children of the English, and can not expect to be so wise and comfortable as they. But you must remember that the Americans have a future before them, and we are not enemies any more. Will you be friends with me, and let me call you my little girl?"

"I shouldn't mind being your little girl, if I could still have the same mamma," was Susie's reply. "Papa is away a great deal, and you could be papa, you know, until he came back."

I made some laughing answer; but, in fact, Susie's frank analysis of the situation poignantly kindled an imagination which stood in no need of stimulus. Ah, if this were the Golden Age, when love never went astray, how happy we might be! But it is not the Golden Age--far from it! Meanwhile, I think I can assert, with a clear conscience, that no dishonorable purpose possessed me. I loved Ethel too profoundly to wish to do her wrong. Yet I may have wished--I did wish--that a kindly Providence might have seen fit to remove the disabilities that controlled us. If a wish could have removed Courtney painlessly to another world, I think I should have wished it. There was something exquisitely touching in Ethel's appearance and manner. She is as pure as any woman that ever lived; but she is a woman! and I felt that, for this day, I had a man's power over her. Occasionally I was conscious that her eyes were resting on my face; when I addressed her, her aspect softened and brightened; she fell into little moods of preoccupation from which she would emerge with a sigh; in many ways she betrayed, without knowing it, the secret that neither of us would mention. I do not mean to imply that she expected me to mention it. A pure woman does not realize the dangers of the world; and that very fact is itself her strongest security against them. But, had I spoken, she would have responded. It was a temptation which I could hardly have believed I could have resisted as I did; but such a woman calls out all that is best and noblest in a man; and, at the time, I was better than I am!

When we were in the brougham again, I said, "If you will allow me, I will drive you to a house I have seen, which belongs to a man with whom I am slightly acquainted. He is on the point of leaving it, but his furniture is still in it, and, as he is himself an artist and a man of taste, it will be worth your while to look at it. He is rather deaf, but that is all the better; we can express our opinions without disturbing him. Perhaps you might arrange to take house and furniture as they stand."

"Whatever you advise, I shall like to do," Ethel answered.

We presently arrived at the house, which was situated in the upper part of the town, a little to the west of Fifth Avenue. It was a comely gabled edifice of red brick, with square bay-windows and a roomy porch. The occupant, Maler, a German, happened to be at home; and on my sending in my card, we were admitted at once, and he came to greet us in the hall in his usual hearty, headlong fashion.

"My good Campbell," he exclaimed, in his blundering English, "very delighted to see you. Ah, dis will be madame, and de little maid! So you are married since some time--I have not know it! Your servant, Madame Campbell. I know--all de artists know--your husband: we wish we could paint how he can--but it is impossible! Ha, ha, ha! not so! Now, I am very pleased you shall see dis house. May I beg de honor of accompany you? First you shall see de studio; dat I call de stomach of de house, eh? because it is most important of all de places, and make de rest of de places live. See, I make dat window be put in--you find no better light in New York. Den you see, here we have de alcove, where Madame Campbell shall sit and make her sewing, while de husband do his work on de easel. How you like dat portiere? I design him myself--oh, yes, I do all here; you keep them if you like; I go to Germany, perhaps not come back after some years, so I leave dem, not so? Now I show you my little chamber of the piano. See, I make an arched ceiling--groined arch, eh?--and I gild him; so I get pretty light and pretty sound, not? Ah! madame, I have not de happiness to be married, but I make my house so, dat if I get me a wife, she find all ready; but no wife come, so I give him over to Herr Campbell and you. Now we mount up-stairs to de bed-rooms, eh?"

In this way he went over the entire house with us. His loud, jolly voice, his resounding laugh, his bustling manner, his heedless, boy- like self-confidence, and his deafness, made it impossible to get in a word of explanation, and, after a few efforts, I gave up the attempt.

"Let him suppose what he likes," I said aside to Ethel, "it can make no difference; he is going away, and you will never see him again. After all these years, it can do no great harm for us to play at being Mr. and Mrs. Campbell for an hour!"

"It is a very beautiful house," she said, tacitly accepting what I had proposed. "It is such a house as I have always dreamed of living in. I shall not care to look at any others. Will you tell him that we--that I will take it just as it stands. You have made this a very pleasant day for me--a very happy day," she added, in a lower tone. "Every room here will be associated with you. You will come here often and see me, will you not? Perhaps, after all, you might use the studio to paint my--or Susie's portrait in."

"I shall inflict myself upon you very often, I have no doubt," was all I ventured to reply. I could not tell her, at that moment, that we must never see each other again. She--after the manner of women--probably supposes that a man's strength is limitless; that he may do with himself and make of himself what he chooses; and she supposes that I could visit her and converse with her day after day, and yet keep my thoughts and my acts within such bounds as would enable me to take Courtney honestly by the hand. But I know too well my own weakness, and I shall leave her while yet I have power to do so. Tomorrow--or soon--I will write to her one last letter, telling her why I go.

Sudden and strange indeed has been this passionate episode in a life which, methought, had done with passion. It has lasted hardly so many hours as I have lived years; and yet, were I to live on into the next century, it would never cease to influence me in all I think and do. I can not solve to my satisfaction this problem-- why two lives should be wasted as ours have been. Courtney could have been happy with another wife, or with no wife at all, perhaps; but, for Ethel and me, there could be no happiness save in each other. But were she free to-day, the separation that has already existed--long though it has been--would only serve to render our future union more blissful and complete. We have learned, by sad experience, the value of a love like ours, and we should know how to give it its fullest and widest expression. But oh! what a blank and chilly road lies before us now!

I drove her back to her hotel; we hardly spoke all the way; my heart was too full, and hers also, I think; though she did not know, as I did, that it was our last interview. It must be our last! Heaven help me to keep that resolution!

Susie was not at all impressed by the pathos of the situation; she babbled all the time, and thus, at all events, afforded us an excuse for our silence. At parting, one incident occurred that may as well be recorded. I had shaken hands with Ethel, speaking a few words of farewell, and allowing her to infer that we might meet again on the morrow; then I turned to Susie, and gave her the kiss which I would have given the world to have had the right to press on her mother's lips. Ethel saw, and, I think, understood. She stooped quickly down, and laid her mouth where mine had been. Through the innocent medium of the child, our hearts met; and then I saw her no more.

May 3d.--Of course, it may not be true, probably it is not; mistakes are so easily made in the first moments of such horror and confusion; the dead come to life, and the living die. Or, at the worst, he may be only wounded or disabled. At all events, I decline to believe, save upon certain evidence, that the poor fellow has actually been killed. Were it to turn out so, I should feel almost like a murderer; for was not I writing, in this very journal, and perhaps at the very moment the accident occurred, that if my wish could send him to another world, I would not spare him?

Later.--I have read all the accounts in the newspapers this morning, and all agree in putting Courtney's name among the killed. There can be no doubt about it any longer; he is dead. When the collision occurred, the car in which he vas riding was thrown across the track, and the other train crashed through it. Judging by the condition of the body when discovered, death must have been nearly instantaneous. Poor Courtney! My conscience is not at ease. Of course, I am not really responsible; that is only imagination. But I begin to suspect that my imagination has been playing me more than one trick lately.

And now, with this new state of affairs so suddenly and terribly brought about, what is to be done? I am as yet scarcely in a condition to reflect calmly; but a voice within me seems to say that something else besides my conscience has been awakened by Courtney's death. Can it be that imagination, dallying with what it took for impossibilities, could so far mislead a man? Well, I shall start at once for the scene of the disaster, and relieve the poor fellow's widow of whatever pain I can. Ethel Courtney a widow! Ah, Ethel! Death sheds a ghastly light upon the idle vagaries of the human heart.

May 15th.--Denver, Colorado.--Magnificent weather and scenery; very different from my own mental scenery and mood at this moment. I am sorely out of spirits; and no wonder, after the reckless and insane emotion of the first days of this month. One pays for such indulgences at my age.

I have been re-reading the foregoing pages of this journal. Was I a fool or a coward, or was I merely intoxicated for eight-and-forty hours? At all events, Courtney's tragic end sobered me, and put what I had been doing in a true light. I am glad my insanity was not permitted to proceed farther than it did; but I have quite enough to reproach myself with as it is. So far as I hare been able to explain the matter to myself, my prime error lay in attributing, in a world subject to constant change, too much permanence to a given state of affairs. The fact that Ethel was the wife of another man seemed to me so fixed and unalterable that I allowed my imagination to play with the picture of what might happen if that unalterable fact were altered. Secure in this fallacy, I worked myself up to the pitch of believing that I was actually and passionately in love with a woman whose inaccessibility was, after all, her most winning attraction. Moreover, by writing down, in this journal, the events and words of the hours we spent together, I confirmed myself in my false persuasion, and probably imported into the record of what we said and did an amount of color and hidden significance that never, as I am now convinced, belonged to it in reality. Deluded by the notion that I was playing with a fancy, I was suddenly aroused to find myself imbrued in facts. The whole episode has profoundly humiliated me, and degraded me in my own esteem.

But I am not at the bottom of the mystery yet. Was I not in love with Ethel? Surely I was, if love be anything. Then why did I not ask her to marry me? Would she have refused me? No. That last look she gave me from under her black veil, when I told her I was going away.... Ah, no, she would not have refused me. Then why did I hesitate? Was not such a marriage precisely what I have always longed for? During all these seven years have I not been bewailing my bachelorhood, and wishing for an Ethel to cheer my solitary fireside with her gracious presence, to be interested in my work and hopes, to interest me in her wifely and maternal ways and aspirations? And when at last all these things were offered me, why did I shrink back and reject them?

Honestly, I can not explain it. Perhaps, if I had never loved her before, I might have loved her this time enough to unite my fate with hers. Or, perhaps--for I may as well speak plainly, since I am speaking to myself--perhaps, by force of habit, I had grown to love, better than love itself, those self-same forlorn conditions and dreary solitudes which I was continually lamenting and praying to be delivered from. What a dismal solution of the problem this would be were it the true one! It amounts to saying that I prefer an empty room, a silent hearth, an old pair of slippers, and a dressing-gown to the love and companionship of a refined and beautiful woman!--that I love even my own discomforts more than the comfort she would give me! It sounds absurd, scandalous, impossible; and yet, if it be not the literal truth, I know not what the truth is. It is amazing that an educated and intelligent man can live to be forty years old and still have come to no better an understanding of himself than I had. Verily, as my old author said, thought is free, but nature is captive, and loveth her chain. Yes, my old author was right.

MY FRIEND PATON.

Mathew Morriss, my father, was a cotton merchant in Liverpool twenty- five years ago--a steady, laborious, clear-headed man, very affectionate and genial in his private intercourse. He was wealthy, and we lived in a sumptuous house in the upper part of the city. This was when I was about ten years old. My father was twice married; I was the child of the first wife, who died when I was very young; my stepmother came five years later. She was the elder of two sisters, both beautiful women. The sister often came to visit us. I remember I liked her better than I liked my stepmother; in fact, I regarded her with that sort of romantic attachment that often is developed in lads of my age. She had golden brown hair and a remarkably sweet voice, and she sang and played in a manner that transported me with delight; for I was already devoted to music. She was of a gentle yet impulsive temperament, easily moved to smiles and tears; she seemed to me the perfection of womankind, and I made no secret of my determination to marry her when I grew up. She used to caress me, and look at me in a dreamy way, and tell me I was the nicest and handsomest boy in the world. "And as soon as you are a year older than I am, John," she would say, "you shall marry me, if you like."

Another frequent visitor at our house at this time was not nearly so much a favorite of mine. This was a German, Adolf Koerner by name, who had been a clerk in my father's concern for a number of years, and had just been admitted junior partner. My father placed every confidence in him, and often declared that he had the best idea of business he had ever met with. This may very likely have been the fact; but to me he appeared simply a tall, grave, taciturn man, of cold manners, speaking with a slight German accent, which I disliked. I suppose he was about thirty-seven years of age, but I always thought of him as older than my father, who was fifty. Another and more valid reason for my disliking Koerner was that he was in the habit of paying a great deal of attention to my ladylove, Miss Juliet Tretherne. I used to upbraid Juliet about encouraging his advances, and I expressed my opinion of him in the plainest language, at which she would smile in a preoccupied wav, and would sometimes draw me to her and kiss me on the forehead. Once she said, "Mr. Koerner is a very noble gentleman; you must not dislike him." This had the effect of making me hate him all the more.

One day I noticed an unusual commotion in the house, and Juliet came downstairs attired in a lovely white dress, with a long veil, and fragrant flowers in her hair. She got into a carriage with my father and stepmother, and drove away. I did not understand what it meant, and no one told me. After they were gone I went into the drawing-room, and, greatly to my surprise, saw there a long table covered with a white cloth and laid out with a profusion of good things to eat and drink in sparkling dishes and decanters. In the middle of the table was a great cake covered with white frosting; the butler was arranging some flowers round it.

"What is that cake for, Curtis?" I asked.

"For the bride, to be sure," said Curtis, without looking up.

"The bride! who is she?" I demanded in astonishment.

"Your aunt Juliet, to be sure!" said Curtis, composedly, stepping back and contemplating his floral arrangement with his head on one side.

I asked no more, but betook myself with all speed to my room, locked the door, flung myself on the bed, and cried to heartbreaking with grief, indignation, and mortification. After a very long time some one tried the door, and a voice--the voice of Juliet--called to me. I made no answer. She began to plead with me; I resisted as long as I could, but finally my affection got the better of my resentment, and I arose and opened the door, hiding my tear-stained face behind my arm. Juliet caught me in her arms and kissed me; tears were running down her own cheeks. How lovely she looked! My heart melted, and I was just on the point of forgiving her when the voice of Koerner became audible from below, calling out "Mrs. Koerner!" I tore myself away from her, and cried passionately, "You don't love me! you love him! go to him!" She looked at me for a moment with a pained expression; then she put her hand in the pocket of her dress and drew out something done up in white paper. "See what I have brought you, you unkind boy," said she. "What is it?" I demanded. "A piece of my wedding-cake," she replied. "Give it me!" said I. She put it in my hand; I ran forward to the head of the stairs, which Koerner was just ascending, dashed the cake in his face, and then rushed back to my own room, whence neither threats nor coaxing availed to draw me forth for the rest of the day.

I never saw Juliet again. She and her husband departed on their wedding-trip that afternoon; it was to take them as far as Germany, for Koerner said that he wished to visit his father and mother, who were still alive, before settling down permanently in Liverpool. Whether they really did so was never discovered. But, about a fortnight later, a dreadful fact came to light. Koerner--the grave and reticent Koerner, whom everybody trusted and thought so highly of--was a thief, and he had gone off with more than half my father's property in his pocket. The blow almost destroyed my father, and my stepmother, too, for that matter, for at first it seemed as though Juliet must have been privy to the crime. This, however, turned out not to have been the case. Her fate must have been all the more terrible on that account; but no news of either of them ever came back to us, and my father would never take any measures to bring Koerner to justice. It was several months before he recovered from the shock sufficiently to take up business again; and then the American Civil War came and completed his ruin. He died, a poor and broken-down man, a year later. My stepmother, who was really an admirable woman, realized whatever property remained to us, took a small house, and sent me to an excellent school, where I was educated for Cambridge. Meanwhile I had been devoting all possible time to music; for I had determined to become a composer, and I was looking forward, after taking my degree, to completing my musical education abroad; but my mother's health was precarious, and, when the time came, she found herself unequal to making the journey, and the change of habits and surroundings that it implied. We lived very quietly in Liverpool for three or four years; then she died, and, after I had settled our affairs, I found myself in possession of a small income and alone in the world. Without loss of time I set out for the Continent.

I went to a German city, where the best musical training was to be had, and made my arrangements to pass several years there. At the banker's, when I went to provide for the regular receipt of my remittances, I met a young American, by name Paton Jeffries. He was from New England, and, I think, a native of the State of Connecticut; his father, he told me, was a distinguished inventor, who had made and lost a considerable fortune in devising a means of promoting sleep by electricity. Paton was studying to be an architect, which, he said, was the coming profession in his country; and it was evident, on a short acquaintance, that he was a fellow of unusual talents--one of those men of whom you say that, come what may, they are always sure to fall on their feet. For my part, I have certainly never met with so active and versatile a spirit. He was a year or so older than I, rather tall than short, lightly but strongly built, with a keen, smiling, subtle face, a finely-developed forehead, light wavy hair, and gray eyes, very penetrating and bright. There was a pleasing kind of eagerness and volubility in his manner of talking, and a slight imperfection, not amounting to a lisp, in his utterance, which imparted a naive charm to his speech. He used expressive and rapid gestures with his hands and arms, and there was a magnetism, a fascination, about the whole man that strongly impressed me. I was at that period much more susceptible of impressions, and prone to yield to them, than I am now. Paton's rattling vivacity, his knowledge of the world, his entertaining talk and stories, his curiosity, enterprise, and audacity, took me by storm; he was my opposite in temperament and character, and it seemed to me that he had most of the advantages on his side. Nevertheless, he professed, and I still believe he felt, a great liking for me, and we speedily came to an agreement to seek a lodging together. On the second day of our search, we found just what we wanted.

It was an old house, on the outskirts of the town, standing by itself, with a small garden behind it. It had formerly been occupied by an Austrian baron, and it was probably not less than two hundred years old. The baron's family had died out, or been dispersed, and now the venerable edifice was let, in the German fashion, in separate floors or *etages*, communicating with a central staircase. Some alterations rendered necessary by this modification had been made, but substantially the house was unchanged. Our apartment comprised four or five rooms on the left of the landing and at the top of the house, which consisted of three stories. The chief room was the parlor, which looked down through a square bow-window on the street. This room was of irregular shape, one end being narrower than the other, and nearly fitting the space at this end was a kind of projecting shelf or mantelpiece (only, of course, there was no fireplace under it, open fireplaces being unknown in Germany), upon which rested an old cracked looking-glass, made in two compartments, the frame of which, black with age and fly-spots, was fastened against the wall. The shelf was supported by two pilasters; but the object of the whole structure was a mystery; so far as appeared, it served no purpose but to support the looking-glass, which might just as well have been suspended from a nail in the wall. Paton, I remember, betrayed a great deal of curiosity about it; and since the consideration of the problem was more in his line of business than in mine, I left it to him. At the opposite end of the room stood a tall earthenware stove. The walls were wainscoted five feet up from the dark polished floor, and were hung with several smoky old paintings, of no great artistic value. The chairs and tables were plain, but very heavy and solid, and of a dark hue like the room. The window was nearly as wide as it was high, and opened laterally from the center on hinges. The other rooms were of the same general appearance, but smaller. We both liked the place, and soon made ourselves very comfortable in it. I hired a piano, and had it conveyed upstairs to the parlor; while Paton disposed his architectural paraphernalia on and in the massive writing-table near the window. Our cooking and other household duties were done for us by the wife of the *portier*, the official corresponding to the French *concierge*, who, in all German houses, attends at the common door, and who, in this case, lived in a couple of musty little closets opening into the lower hall, and eked out his official salary by cobbling shoes. He was an odd, grotesque humorist, of most ungainly exterior, black haired and bearded, with a squint, a squab nose, and a short but very powerful figure. Dirty he was beyond belief, and he was abominably fragrant of vile tobacco. For my part, I could not endure this fellow; but Paton, who had much more of what he called human nature in him than I had, established friendly relations with him at once, and reported that he found him very amusing. It was characteristic of Paton that, though he knew much less about the German language than I did, he could understand and make himself understood in it much better; and, when we were in company, it was always he who did the talking.

It would never have occurred to me to wonder, much less to inquire, who might be the occupants of the other *etages*; but Paton was more enterprising, and before we had been settled three days in our new quarters, he had gathered from his friend the portier, and from other sources, all the obtainable information on the subject. The information was of no particular interest, however, except as regarded the persons who dwelt on the floor immediately below us. They were two--an old man and a young woman, supposed to be his daughter. They had been living here several years--from before the time, indeed, that the portier had occupied his present position. In all these years the old man was known to have been out of his room only twice. He was certainly an eccentric person, and was said to be a miser and extremely wealthy. The portier further averred that his property--except such small portion of it as was invested and on the income of which he lived--was realized in the form of diamonds and other precious stones, which, for greater security, he always carried, waking or sleeping, in a small leathern bag, fastened round his neck by a fine steel chain. His daughter was scarcely less a mystery than he, for, though she went out as often as twice or thrice a week, she was always closely veiled, and her figure was so disguised by the long cloak she wore that it was impossible to say whether she were graceful or deformed, beautiful or ugly. The balance of belief, however, was against her being attractive in any respect. The name by which the old miser was known was Kragendorf; but, as the portier sagaciously remarked, there was no knowing, in such cases, whether the name a man bore was his own or somebody's else.

This Kragendorf mystery was another source of apparently inexhaustible interest to Paton, who was fertile in suggestions as to how it might be explained or penetrated. I believe he and the portier talked it over at great length, but, so far as I am aware, without arriving at any solution. I took little heed of the matter, being now fully absorbed in my studies; and it is to be hoped that Herr Kragendorf was not of a nervous temperament, otherwise he must have inveighed profanely against the constant piano-practice that went on over his head. I also had a violin, on which I flattered myself I could perform with a good deal of expression, and by and by, in the long, still evenings--it was November, but the temperature was still mild--I got into the habit of strolling along the less frequented streets, with my violin under my shoulder, drawing from it whatever music my heart desired. Occasionally I would pause at some convenient spot, lean against a wall, and give myself up to improvisation. At such times a little cluster of auditors would gradually collect in front of me, listening for the most part silently, or occasionally giving vent to low grunts and interjections of approval. One evening, I remember, a young woman joined the group, though keeping somewhat in the background; she listened intently, and after a time gradually turned her face toward me, unconsciously as it were; and the light of a street-lamp at a little distance revealed a countenance youthful, pale, sad, and exquisitely beautiful. It impressed me as with a vague reminiscence of something I had seen or imagined--some pictured face, perhaps, caught in a glance and never to be identified. Her eyes finally met mine; I stopped playing. She started, gave me an alarmed look, and, gliding swiftly away, disappeared. I could not forget this incident; it haunted me strangely and persistently. Many a time thereafter I revisited the same spot, and drew together other audiences, but the delicate girl with the dark-blue eyes and the tender, sensitive mouth, was never again among them.

It was at this epoch, I think, that the inexhaustible Paton made a discovery. From my point of view it was not a discovery of any moment; but, as usual, he took interest in it enough for both of us. It appeared that, in attempting to doctor the crack in the old looking- glass, a large piece of the plate had got loose, and come away in his hands; and in the space behind he had detected a paper, carefully folded and tied up with a piece of faded ribbon. Paton was never in the habit of hampering himself with fine-drawn scruples, and he had no hesitation in opening the folded paper and spreading it out on the table. Judging from the glance I gave it, it seemed to be a confused and abstruse mixture of irregular geometrical figures and cramped German chirography. But Paton set to work upon it with as much concentration as if it had been a recipe for the Philosopher's Stone; he reproduced the lines and angles on fresh paper, and labored over the writing with a magnifying-glass and a dictionary. At times he would mutter indistinctly to himself, lift his eyebrows, nod or shake his head, bite his lips, and rub his forehead, and anon fall to work again with fresh vigor. At last he leaned back in his chair, thumped his hand on the table, and laughed.

"Got it!" he exclaimed. "Say, John, old boy, I've got it! and it's the most curious old thing ever you saw in your life!"

"Something in analytical geometry, isn't it?" said I, turning round on my piano-stool.

"Analytical pudding's end! It's a plan of a house, my boy, and, what's more, of this very house we're in! That's a find, and no mistake! These are the descriptions and explanations--these bits of writing. It's a perfect labyrinth of Crete! Udolpho was nothing to it!"

"Well, I suppose it isn't of much value except as a curiosity?"

"Don't be too sure of that, John, my boy! Who knows but there's a treasure concealed somewhere in this house? or a skeleton in a secret chamber! This old paper may make our fortune yet!"

"The treasure wouldn't belong to us if we found it; and, besides, we can't make explorations beyond our own premises, and we know what's in them already."

"Do we? Did we know what was behind the looking-glass? Did you never hear of sliding panels, and private passages, and concealed staircases? Where's your imagination, man? But you don't need imagination--here it is in black and white!"

As he spoke, he pointed to a part of the plan; but, as I was stooping to examine it, he seemed to change his mind.

"No matter," he exclaimed, suddenly folding up the paper and rising from his chair. "You're not an architect, and you can't be expected to go in for these things. No; there's no practical use in it, of course. But secret passages were always a hobby of mine. Well, what are you going to do this evening? Come over to the cafe and have a game of billiards!"

"No; I shall go to bed early to-night."

"You sleep too much," said Paton. "Everybody does, if my father, instead of inventing a way of promoting sleep, had invented a way of doing without it, he'd have been the richest man in America to-day. However, do as you like. I sha'n't be back till late."

He put on his hat and sallied forth with a cigar in his mouth. Paton was of rather a convivial turn; he liked to have a good time, as he called it; and, indeed, he seemed to think that the chief end of man was to get money enough to have a good time continually, a sort of good eternity. His head was strong, and he could stand a great deal of liquor; and I have seen him sip and savor a glass of raw brandy or whisky as another man would a glass of Madeira. In this, and the other phases of his life about town, I had no participation, being constitutionally as well as by training averse therefrom; and he, on the other hand, would never have listened to my sage advice to modify his loose habits. Our companionship was apart from these things; and, as I have said, I found in him a good deal that I could sympathize with, without approaching the moralities.

That night, after I had been for some time asleep, I awoke and found myself listening to a scratching and shoving noise that seemed quite unaccountable. By-and-by it made me uneasy. I got up and went toward the parlor, from which the noise proceeded. On reaching the doorway, I saw Paton on his knees before one of the pilasters in the narrow end of the room; a candle was on the floor beside him, and he was busily at work at something, though what it was I could not make out. The creak of the threshold under my foot caused him to look round. He started violently, and sprang to his feet.

"Oh! it's you, is it?" he said, after a moment. "Great Scott! how you scared me! I was--I dropped a bit of money hereabouts, and I was scraping about to find it. No matter--it wasn't much! Sorry I disturbed you, old boy." And, laughing, he picked up his candle and went into his own room.

From this time there was a change vaguely perceptible in our mutual relations; we chatted together less than before, and did not see so much of each other. Paton was apt to be out when I was at home, and generally sat up after I was abed. He seemed to be busy about something--something connected with his profession, I judged; but, contrary to his former custom, he made no attempt to interest me in it. To tell the truth, I had begun to realize that our different tastes and pursuits must lead us further and further apart, and that our separation could be only a question of time. Paton was a materialist, and inclined to challenge all the laws and convictions that mankind has instituted and adopted; there was no limit to his radicalism. For example, on coming in one day, I found him with a curious antique poniard in his hands, which he had probably bought in some old curiosity shop. At first I fancied he meant to conceal it; but, if so, he changed his mind.

"What do you think of that?" he said, holding it out to me. "There's a solution of continuity for you! Mind you don't prick yourself! It's poisoned up to the hilt!"

"What do you want of such a thing?" I asked.

"Well, killing began with Cain, and isn't likely to go out of fashion in our day. I might find it convenient to give one of my friends--you, for instance--a reminder of his mortality some time. You'll say murder is immoral. Bless you, man, we never could do without it! No man dies before his time, and some one dies every day that some one else may live."

This was said in a jocose way, and, of course, Paton did not mean it. But it affected me unpleasantly nevertheless.

As I was washing my hands in my room, I happened to look out of my window, which commanded a view of the garden at the back of the house. It was an hour after sunset, and the garden was nearly dark; but I caught a movement of something below, and, looking more closely, I recognized the ugly figure of the portier. He seemed to be tying something to the end of a long slender pole, like a gigantic fishing- rod; and presently he advanced beneath my window, and raised the pole as high as it would go against the wall of the house. The point he touched was the sill of the window below mine--probably that of the bedroom of Herr Kragendorf. At this juncture the portier seemed to be startled at something--possibly he saw me at my window; at all events, he lowered his pole and disappeared in the house.

The next day Paton made an announcement that took me by surprise. He said he had made up his mind to quit Germany, and that very shortly. He mentioned having received letters from home, and declared he had got, or should soon have got, all he wanted out of this country. "I'm going to stop paying money for instruction," he said, "and begin to earn it by work. I shall stay another week, but then I'm off. Too slow here for me! I want to be in the midst of things, using my time."

I did not attempt to dissuade him; in fact, my first feeling was rather one of relief; and this Paton, with his quick preceptions, was probably aware of.

"Own up, old boy!" he said, laughing; "you'll be able to endure my absence. And yet you needn't think of me as worse than anybody else. If everybody were musicians and moralists, it would be nice, no doubt; but one might get tired of it in time, and then what would you do? You must give the scamps and adventurers their innings, after all! They may not do much good, but they give the other fellows occupation. I was born without my leave being asked, and I may act as suits me without asking anybody's leave."

This was said on a certain bright morning after our first fall of snow; the tiled roofs of the houses were whitened with it, it cushioned the window-sills, and spread a sparkling blankness over the garden. In the streets it was already melting, and people were slipping and splashing on the wet and glistening pavements. After gazing out at this scene for a while, in a mood of unwonted thoughtfulness, Paton yawned, stretched himself, and declared his intention of taking a stroll before dinner. Accordingly he lit a cigar and went forth. I watched him go down the street and turn the corner.

An hour afterward, just when dinner was on the table, I heard an unusual noise and shuffling on the stairs, and a heavy knock on the door. I opened it, and saw four men bearing on a pallet the form of my friend Paton. A police officer accompanied them. They brought Paton in, and laid him on his bed. The officer told me briefly what had happened, gave me certain directions, and, saying that a surgeon would arrive immediately, he departed with the four men tramping behind him.

Paton had slipped in going across the street, and a tramway car had run over him. He was not dead, though almost speechless; but his injuries were such that it was impossible that he should recover. He kept his eyes upon me; they were as bright as ever, though his face was deadly pale. He seemed to be trying to read my thoughts--to find out my feeling about him, and my opinion of his condition. I was terribly shocked and grieved, and my face no doubt showed it. By-and-by I saw his lips move, and bent down to listen.

"Confounded nuisance!" he whispered faintly in my car. "It's all right, though; I'm not going to die this time. I've got something to do, and I'm going to do it--devil take me if I don't!"

He was unable to say more, and soon after the surgeon came in. He made an examination, and it was evident that he had no hope. His shrug of the shoulders was not lost upon Paton, who frowned, and made a defiant movement of the lip. But presently he said to me, still in the same whisper, "John, if that old fool should be right--he won't be, but in case of accidents--you must take charge of my things--the papers, and all. I'll make you heir of my expectations! Write out a declaration to that effect: I can sign my name; and he'll be witness."

I did as he directed, and having explained to the surgeon the nature of the document, I put the pen in Paton's hand; but was obliged to guide his hand with my own in order to make an intelligible signature. The surgeon signed below, and Paton seemed satisfied. He closed his eyes; his sufferings appeared to be very slight. But, even while I was looking at him, a change came over his face--a deadly change. His eyes opened; they were no longer bright, but sunken and dull. He gave me a dusky look--whether of rage, of fear, or of entreaty, I could not tell. His lips parted, and a voice made itself audible; not like his own voice, but husky and discordant. "I'm going," it said. "But look out for me.... Do it yourself!"

"Der Herr ist todt" (the man is dead), said the surgeon the next minute.

It was true. Paton had gone out of this life at an hour's warning. What purpose or desire his last words indicated, there was nothing to show. He was dead; and yet I could hardly believe that it was so. He had been so much alive; so full of schemes and enterprises. Nothing now was left but that crushed and haggard figure, stiffening on the bed; nothing, at least, that mortal senses could take cognizance of. It was a strange thought.

Paton's funeral took place a few days afterward. I returned from the graveyard weary in body and mind. At the door of the house stood the portier, who nodded to me, and said,

"A very sad thing to happen, worthy sir; but so it is in the world. Of all the occupants of this house, one would have said the one least likely to be dead to-day was Herr Jeffries. Heh! if I had been the good Providence, I would have made away with the old gentleman of the *etage* below, who is of no use to anybody."

This, for lack of a better, was Paton's funeral oration. I climbed the three flights of stairs and let myself into our apartment--mine exclusively now. The place was terribly lonely; much more so than if Paton had been alive anywhere in the world. But he was dead; and, if his own philosophy were true, he was annihilated. But it was not true! How distinct and minute was my recollection of him--his look, his gestures, the tones of his voice. I could almost see him before me; my memory of him dead seemed clearer than when he was alive. In that invisible world of the mind was he not living still, and perhaps not far away.

I sat down at the table where he had been wont to work, and unlocked the drawers in which he kept his papers. These, or some of them, I took out and spread before me. But I found it impossible, as yet, to concentrate my attention upon them; I pushed back my chair, and, rising, went to the piano. Here I remained for perhaps a couple of hours, striking the vague chords that echo wandering thoughts. I was trying to banish this haunting image of Paton from my mind, and at length I partly succeeded.

All at once, however, the impression of him (as I may call it) came back with a force and vividness that startled me. I stopped playing, and sat for a minute perfectly still. I felt that Paton was in the room; that if I looked round I should see him. I however restrained myself from looking round with all the strength of my will--wherefore I know not. What I felt was not fear, but the conviction that I was on the brink of a fearful and unprecedented experience--an experience that would not leave me as it found me. This strange struggle with myself taxed all my powers; the sweat started out on my forehead. At last the moment came when I could struggle no longer. I laid my hand on the keyboard, and pushed myself round on the stool. There was a momentary dazzle before my eyes, and after that I saw plainly. My hand, striking the keys, had produced a jarring discord; and while this was yet tingling in my ears, Paton, who was sitting in his old place at the table, with his back toward me, faced about in his chair, and his eyes met mine. I thought he smiled.

My excitement was past, and was succeeded by a dead calm. I examined him critically. His appearance was much the same as when in life; nay, he was even more like himself than before. The subtle or crafty expression which had always been discernible in his features was now intensified, and there was something wild and covertly fierce in the shining of his gray eyes, something that his smile was unable to disguise. What was human and genial in my former friend had passed away, and what remained was evil--the kind of evil that I now perceived to have been at the base of his nature. It was a revelation of character terrible in its naked completeness. I knew at a glance that Paton must always have been a far more wicked man that I had ever imagined; and in his present state all the remains of goodness had been stripped away, and nothing but wickedness was left.

I felt impelled, by an impulse for which I could not account, to approach the table and examine the papers once more; and now it entered into my mind to perceive a certain method and meaning in them that had been hidden from me before.

It was as though I were looking at them through Paton's intelligence, and with his memory. He had in some way ceased to be visible to me; but I became aware that he wished me to sit down in his chair, and I did so. Under his guidance, and in obedience to a will that seemed to be my own, and yet was in direct opposition to my real will, I began a systematic study of the papers. Paton, meanwhile, remained close to me, though I could no longer see him; but I felt the gaze of his fierce, shining eyes, and his crafty, evil smile. I soon obtained a tolerable insight into what the papers meant, and what was the scheme in which Paton had been so much absorbed at the time of his death, and which he had been so loath to abandon.

It was a wicked and cruel scheme, worked out to the smallest particular. But, though I understood its hideousness intellectually, it aroused in mo no corresponding emotion; my sensitiveness to right arid wrong seemed stupefied or inoperative. I could say, "This is wicked," but I could not awaken in myself a horror of committing the wickedness; and, moreover, I knew that, if the influence Paton was able to exercise over me continued, I must in due time commit it.

Presently I became aware, or, to speak more accurately, I seemed to remember, that there was something in Paton's room which it was incumbent on me to procure. I went thither, lifted up a corner of the rag between the bed and the stove, and beheld, in an aperture in the floor, of the existence of which I had till now known nothing, the antique poisoned dagger that Paton had showed me a few weeks before, and which I had not seen since then. I brought it back to the sitting- room, put it in a drawer of the table, and locked the drawer, at the same time making a mental note to the effect that I should reopen the drawer at a certain hour of the night and take the dagger out. All this while Paton was close at hand, though not visible to sight; but I had a sort of inner perception of his presence and movements. All at once, at about the hour of sunset, I saw him again; he moved toward the looking-glass at the narrow end of the room, laid his hand upon one of the pilasters, glanced at me over his shoulder, and immediately seemed to stoop down. As I sat, the edge of the table hid him from sight. I stood up and looked across. He was not there; and a kind of reaction of my nerves informed me that he was gone absolutely, for the time.

This reaction produced a lassitude impossible to describe; it was overpowering, and I had no choice but to yield to it. I dropped back in my chair, leaned forward on the table, and instantly fell into a heavy sleep, or stupor.

I awoke abruptly, with a sensation as if a hand had been laid on my shoulder. It was night, and I knew that the hour I had noted in my mind was at hand. I opened the drawer and took out the dagger, which I put in my pocket. The house was quite silent. A shiver passed through me. I was aware that Paton was standing at the narrow end of the room, waiting for me: Yes--there he was, or the impression of him in my brain--what did it matter? I arose mechanically and walked toward him. He had no need to direct me: I knew all there was to do, and how to do it. I knelt on the floor, laid my shoulder against the pilaster, and pushed it laterally. It moved aside on a pivot, disclosing an iron ring let into the floor. I laid hold of this ring, and lifted. A section of the floor came up, and I saw a sort of ladder descending perpendicularly into darkness. Down the ladder Paton went, and I followed him. Arrived at the bottom, I turned to the left, led by an instinct or a fascination; passed along a passage barely wide enough to admit me, until I came against a smooth, hard surface. I passed my hand over it until I touched a knob or catch, which I pressed, and the surface gave way before me like a door. I stumbled forward, and found myself in a room of what was doubtless Herr Kragendorf's apartment. A keen, cold air smote against my face; and with it came a sudden influx of strength and self-possession. I felt that, for a moment at least, the fatal influence of Paton upon me was broken. But what was that sound of a struggle--those cries and gasps, that seemed to come from an adjoining room?

I sprang forward, opened a door, and beheld a tall old man, with white hair and beard, in the grasp of a ruffian whom I at once recognized as the portier. A broken window showed how he had effected his entrance. One hand held the old man by the throat; in the other was a knife, which he was prevented from using by a young woman, who had flung herself upon him in such a way as to trammel his movements. In another moment, however, he would have shaken her off.

But that moment was not allowed him. I seized him with a strength that amazed myself--a strength which never came upon me before or since. The conflict lasted but a breath or two; I hurled him to the floor, and, as he fell, his right arm was doubled under him, and the knife which he held entered his back beneath the left shoulder-blade. When I rose up from the whirl and fury of the struggle, I saw the old man reclining exhausted on the bosom of the girl. I knew him, despite his white hair and beard. And the face that bent so lovingly above him was the face that had looked into mine that night on the street--the face of the blue-eyed maiden--of a younger and a lovelier Juliet! As I gazed, there came a thundering summons at the door, and the police entered.

*   *   *   *   *

My poor uncle Koerner had not prospered after his great stroke of roguery. His wife had died of a broken heart, after giving birth to a daughter, and his stolen riches had vanished almost as rapidly as they were acquired. He had at last settled down with his daughter in this old house. The treasure in the leathern bag, though a treasure to him, was not of a nature to excite general cupidity. It consisted, not of precious stones, but of relics of his dead wife--her rings, a lock of her hair, her letters, a miniature of her in a gold case. These poor keepsakes, and his daughter, had been the only solace of his lonely and remorseful life.

It was uncertain whether Paton and the portier had planned the robbery together, or separately, and in ignorance of each other's purpose. Nor can I tell whether my disembodied visitor came to me with good or with evil intent. Wicked spirits, even when they seem to have power to carry out their purposes, are perhaps only permitted to do so, so far as is consistent with an overruling good of which they know nothing. Certainly, if I had not descended the secret passage, Koerner would have been killed, and perhaps my Juliet likewise--the mother of my children. But should I have been led on to stab him myself, with the poisoned dagger, had the portier not been there? Juliet smiles and says No, and I am glad to agree with her. But I have never since then found that anniversary upon me, without a shudder of awe, and a dark thought of Paton Jeffries.

THE END.

The Codes Of Hammurabi And Moses
W. W. Davies

QTY

The discovery of the Hammurabi Code is one of the greatest achievements of archaeology, and is of paramount interest, not only to the student of the Bible, but also to all those interested in ancient history...

Religion   **ISBN:** *1-59462-338-4*   **Pages:132**
MSRP $12.95

The Theory of Moral Sentiments
Adam Smith

QTY

This work from 1749. contains original theories of conscience amd moral judgment and it is the foundation for systemof morals.

Philosophy   **ISBN:** *1-59462-777-0*   **Pages:536**
MSRP $19.95

Jessica's First Prayer
Hesba Stretton

QTY

In a screened and secluded corner of one of the many railway-bridges which span the streets of London there could be seen a few years ago, from five o'clock every morning until half past eight, a tidily set-out coffee-stall, consisting of a trestle and board, upon which stood two large tin cans, with a small fire of charcoal burning under each so as to keep the coffee boiling during the early hours of the morning when the work-people were thronging into the city on their way to their daily toil...

Childrens   **ISBN:** *1-59462-373-2*   **Pages:84**
MSRP $9.95

My Life and Work
Henry Ford

QTY

Henry Ford revolutionized the world with his implementation of mass production for the Model T automobile. Gain valuable business insight into his life and work with his own auto-biography... "We have only started on our development of our country we have not as yet, with all our talk of wonderful progress, done more than scratch the surface. The progress has been wonderful enough but..."

Biographies/   **ISBN:** *1-59462-198-5*   **Pages:300**
MSRP $21.95

The Art of Cross-Examination
Francis Wellman

QTY

I presume it is the experience of every author, after his first book is published upon an important subject, to be almost overwhelmed with a wealth of ideas and illustrations which could readily have been included in his book, and which to his own mind, at least, seem to make a second edition inevitable. Such certainly was the case with me; and when the first edition had reached its sixth impression in five months, I rejoiced to learn that it seemed to my publishers that the book had met with a sufficiently favorable reception to justify a second and considerably enlarged edition. ..

Reference   ISBN: *1-59462-647-2*

Pages:412

MSRP $19.95

On the Duty of Civil Disobedience
Henry David Thoreau

QTY

Thoreau wrote his famous essay, On the Duty of Civil Disobedience, as a protest against an unjust but popular war and the immoral but popular institution of slave-owning. He did more than write—he declined to pay his taxes, and was hauled off to gaol in consequence. Who can say how much this refusal of his hastened the end of the war and of slavery ?

Law   ISBN: *1-59462-747-9*

Pages:48

MSRP $7.45

Dream Psychology Psychoanalysis for Beginners
Sigmund Freud

QTY

Sigmund Freud, born Sigismund Schlomo Freud (May 6, 1856 - September 23, 1939), was a Jewish-Austrian neurologist and psychiatrist who co-founded the psychoanalytic school of psychology. Freud is best known for his theories of the unconscious mind, especially involving the mechanism of repression; his redefinition of sexual desire as mobile and directed towards a wide variety of objects; and his therapeutic techniques, especially his understanding of transference in the therapeutic relationship and the presumed value of dreams as sources of insight into unconscious desires.

Psychology   ISBN: *1-59462-905-6*

Pages:196

MSRP $15.45

The Miracle of Right Thought
Orison Swett Marden

QTY

Believe with all of your heart that you will do what you were made to do. When the mind has once formed the habit of holding cheerful, happy, prosperous pictures, it will not be easy to form the opposite habit. It does not matter how improbable or how far away this realization may see, or how dark the prospects may be, if we visualize them as best we can, as vividly as possible, hold tenaciously to them and vigorously struggle to attain them, they will gradually become actualized, realized in the life. But a desire, a longing without endeavor, a yearning abandoned or held indifferently will vanish without realization.

Pages:360

Self Help   ISBN: *1-59462-644-8*

MSRP $25.45

QTY

The Rosicrucian Cosmo-Conception Mystic Christianity *by Max Heindel*　　ISBN: *1-59462-188-8*　**$38.95**
The Rosicrucian Cosmo-conception is not dogmatic, neither does it appeal to any other authority than the reason of the student. It is: not controversial, but is: sent forth in the, hope that it may help to clear...　　New Age/Religion Pages 646

Abandonment To Divine Providence *by Jean-Pierre de Caussade*　　ISBN: *1-59462-228-0*　**$25.95**
"The Rev. Jean Pierre de Caussade was one of the most remarkable spiritual writers of the Society of Jesus in France in the 18th Century. His death took place at Toulouse in 1751. His works have gone through many editions and have been republished...　　Inspirational/Religion Pages 400

Mental Chemistry *by Charles Haanel*　　ISBN: *1-59462-192-6*　**$23.95**
Mental Chemistry allows the change of material conditions by combining and appropriately utilizing the power of the mind. Much like applied chemistry creates something new and unique out of careful combinations of chemicals the mastery of mental chemistry...　　New Age Pages 354

The Letters of Robert Browning and Elizabeth Barret Barrett 1845-1846 vol II　　ISBN: *1-59462-193-4*　**$35.95**
by Robert Browning and Elizabeth Barrett　　Biographies Pages 596

Gleanings In Genesis (volume I) *by Arthur W. Pink*　　ISBN: *1-59462-130-6*　**$27.45**
Appropriately has Genesis been termed "the seed plot of the Bible" for in it we have, in germ form, almost all of the great doctrines which are afterwards fully developed in the books of Scripture which follow...　　Religion/Inspirational Pages 420

The Master Key *by L. W. de Laurence*　　ISBN: *1-59462-001-6*　**$30.95**
In no branch of human knowledge has there been a more lively increase of the spirit of research during the past few years than in the study of Psychology, Concentration and Mental Discipline. The requests for authentic lessons in Thought Control, Mental Discipline and...　　New Age/Business Pages 422

The Lesser Key Of Solomon Goetia *by L. W. de Laurence*　　ISBN: *1-59462-092-X*　**$9.95**
This translation of the first book of the "Lernegton" which is now for the first time made accessible to students of Talismanic Magic was done, after careful collation and edition, from numerous Ancient Manuscripts in Hebrew, Latin, and French...　　New Age/Occult Pages 92

Rubaiyat Of Omar Khayyam *by Edward Fitzgerald*　　ISBN: *1-59462-332-5*　**$13.95**
Edward Fitzgerald, whom the world has already learned, in spite of his own efforts to remain within the shadow of anonymity, to look upon as one of the rarest poets of the century, was born at Bredfield, in Suffolk, on the 31st of March, 1809. He was the third son of John Purcell...　　Music Pages 172

Ancient Law *by Henry Maine*　　ISBN: *1-59462-128-4*　**$29.95**
The chief object of the following pages is to indicate some of the earliest ideas of mankind, as they are reflected in Ancient Law, and to point out the relation of those ideas to modern thought.　　Religion/History Pages 452

Far-Away Stories *by William J. Locke*　　ISBN: *1-59462-129-2*　**$19.45**
"Good wine needs no bush, but a collection of mixed vintages does. And this book is just such a collection. Some of the stories I do not want to remain buried for ever in the museum files of dead magazine-numbers an author's not unpardonable vanity..."　　Fiction Pages 272

Life of David Crockett *by David Crockett*　　ISBN: *1-59462-250-7*　**$27.45**
"Colonel David Crockett was one of the most remarkable men of the times in which he lived. Born in humble life, but gifted with a strong will, an indomitable courage, and unremitting perseverance...　　Biographies/New Age Pages 424

Lip-Reading *by Edward Nitchie*　　ISBN: *1-59462-206-X*　**$25.95**
Edward B. Nitchie, founder of the New York School for the Hard of Hearing, now the Nitchie School of Lip-Reading, Inc, wrote "LIP-READING Principles and Practice". The development and perfecting of this meritorious work on lip-reading was an undertaking...　　How-to Pages 400

A Handbook of Suggestive Therapeutics, Applied Hypnotism, Psychic Science　　ISBN: *1-59462-214-0*　**$24.95**
by Henry Munro　　Health/New Age/Health/Self-help Pages 376

A Doll's House: and Two Other Plays *by Henrik Ibsen*　　ISBN: *1-59462-112-8*　**$19.95**
Henrik Ibsen created this classic when in revolutionary 1848 Rome. Introducing some striking concepts in playwriting for the realist genre, this play has been studied the world over.　　Fiction/Classics/Plays 308

The Light of Asia *by sir Edwin Arnold*　　ISBN: *1-59462-204-3*　**$13.95**
In this poetic masterpiece, Edwin Arnold describes the life and teachings of Buddha. The man who was to become known as Buddha to the world was born as Prince Gautama of India but he rejected the worldly riches and abandoned the reigns of power when...　　Religion/History/Biographies Pages 170

The Complete Works of Guy de Maupassant *by Guy de Maupassant*　　ISBN: *1-59462-157-8*　**$16.95**
"For days and days, nights and nights, I had dreamed of that first kiss which was to consecrate our engagement, and I knew not on what spot I should put my lips..."　　Fiction/Classics Pages 240

The Art of Cross-Examination *by Francis L. Wellman*　　ISBN: *1-59462-309-0*　**$26.95**
Written by a renowned trial lawyer, Wellman imparts his experience and uses case studies to explain how to use psychology to extract desired information through questioning.　　How-to/Science/Reference Pages 408

Answered or Unanswered? *by Louisa Vaughan*　　ISBN: *1-59462-248-5*　**$10.95**
Miracles of Faith in China　　Religion Pages 112

The Edinburgh Lectures on Mental Science (1909) *by Thomas*　　ISBN: *1-59462-008-3*　**$11.95**
This book contains the substance of a course of lectures recently given by the writer in the Queen Street Hail, Edinburgh. Its purpose is to indicate the Natural Principles governing the relation between Mental Action and Material Conditions...　　New Age/Psychology Pages 148

Ayesha *by H. Rider Haggard*　　ISBN: *1-59462-301-5*　**$24.95**
Verily and indeed it is the unexpected that happens! Probably if there was one person upon the earth from whom the Editor of this, and of a certain previous history, did not expect to hear again...　　Classics Pages 380

Ayala's Angel *by Anthony Trollope*　　ISBN: *1-59462-352-X*　**$29.95**
The two girls were both pretty, but Lucy who was twenty-one who supposed to be simple and comparatively unattractive, whereas Ayala was credited, as her Bombwhat romantic name might show, with poetic charm and a taste for romance. Ayala when her father died was nineteen...　　Fiction Pages 484

The American Commonwealth *by James Bryce*　　ISBN: *1-59462-286-8*　**$34.45**
An interpretation of American democratic political theory. It examines political mechanics and society from the perspective of Scotsman James Bryce　　Politics Pages 572

Stories of the Pilgrims *by Margaret P. Pumphrey*　　ISBN: *1-59462-116-0*　**$17.95**
This book explores pilgrims religious oppression in England as well as their escape to Holland and eventual crossing to America on the Mayflower, and their early days in New England...　　History Pages 268

QTY

The Fasting Cure *by Sinclair Upton*   ISBN: *1-59462-222-1*   **$13.95**
In the Cosmopolitan Magazine for May, 1910, and in the Contemporary Review (London) for April, 1910, I published an article dealing with my experi-
ences in fasting. I have written a great many magazine articles, but never one which attracted so much attention... New Age/Self Help/Health Pages 164

Hebrew Astrology *by Sepharial*   ISBN: *1-59462-308-2*   **$13.45**
In these days of advanced thinking it is a matter of common observation that we have left many of the old landmarks behind and that we are now pressing
forward to greater heights and to a wider horizon than that which represented the mind-content of our progenitors...   Astrology Pages 144

Thought Vibration or The Law of Attraction in the Thought World   ISBN: *1-59462-127-6*   **$12.95**

by William Walker Atkinson   *Psychology/Religion Pages 144*

Optimism *by Helen Keller*   ISBN: *1-59462-108-X*   **$15.95**
Helen Keller was blind, deaf, and mute since 19 months old, yet famously learned how to overcome these handicaps, communicate with the world, and
spread her lectures promoting optimism. An inspiring read for everyone...   Biographies/Inspirational Pages 84

Sara Crewe *by Frances Burnett*   ISBN: *1-59462-360-0*   **$9.45**
In the first place, Miss Minchin lived in London. Her home was a large, dull, tall one, in a large, dull square, where all the houses were alike, and all the
sparrows were alike, and where all the door-knockers made the same heavy sound...   Childrens/Classic Pages 88

The Autobiography of Benjamin Franklin *by Benjamin Franklin*   ISBN: *1-59462-135-7*   **$24.95**
The Autobiography of Benjamin Franklin has probably been more extensively read than any other American historical work, and no other book of its kind
has had such ups and downs of fortune. Franklin lived for many years in England, where he was agent...   Biographies/History Pages 332

Name	
Email	
Telephone	
Address	
City, State ZIP	

☐ **Credit Card**   ☐ **Check / Money Order**

Credit Card Number	
Expiration Date	
Signature	

Please Mail to: Book Jungle
PO Box 2226
Champaign, IL 61825
or Fax to: 630-214-0564

ORDERING INFORMATION

web*: www.bookjungle.com*
email*: sales@bookjungle.com*
fax*: 630-214-0564*
mail*: Book Jungle PO Box 2226 Champaign, IL 61825*
or PayPal *to sales@bookjungle.com*

Please contact us for bulk discounts

DIRECT-ORDER TERMS

**20% Discount if You Order
Two or More Books**
Free Domestic Shipping!
Accepted: Master Card, Visa,
Discover, American Express

www.ingramcontent.com/pod-product-compliance
Lightning Source LLC
Chambersburg PA
CBHW082014170626
46817CB00009B/3100

* 9 7 8 1 4 3 8 5 3 7 3 5 1 *